THE ACTRESS

The Curious Case of Cordelia Wainwright

Kimberly J.M. Wilson

Author Bio

Kimberly J.M. Wilson is an American author living in Cincinnati, Ohio. When she is not writing fiction, she is a history professor.

She enjoys reading, writing, gaming, drinking beer, and hanging out with family and friends. While she has traveled to several countries, her fervent wish is to go to Australia to meet the fine Aussie ladies who first supported her and Cordelia.

Bella Books, Inc.
P.O. Box 10543
Tallahassee, FL 32302

Previously self-published - 2024
Bella Books First Edition - 2025

Cover Designer: SJ Hardy
Cover Author Photo: Britt/Learn To Fly Photography

ISBN: 978-1-64247-690-3

THE ACTRESS

The Curious Case of Cordelia Wainwright

Kimberly J.M. Wilson

BELLA
BOOKS

Acknowledgment

The writings of William Shakespeare were the inspiration for this book.

This book is dedicated to:
My Mother, Louann Begley
My first reader and part-time therapist, Toni Berliner
My greatest teacher, Elizabeth Bookser Barkley
My avid supporters, Lyn, Glenda, Erin & Beverly
The Cincinnati Writers Project
And, of course, all of the Bartlebys of the world.

"Loneliness is the perfect companion. It neither speaks, expects anything in return, nor makes any demands."
                                              -Cordelia Anne Wainwright

Part I

Aubrey

CHAPTER ONE

"Bartleby & Pompey"

Feb. 21, 2017: Los Angeles, CA

"So, is 2017 the year that you finally get what you most covet? Do you agree with the critics that *Solace Alone* is your greatest role?"

Why does this overly-tanned Miss Universe reject always ask me the same fucking question? Does she not understand how dangerous skin cancer is? It kills nearly 8,000 people every year. Of course not; she is not even a real journalist—she probably does not even watch what passes for news on her network.

And, look, there is that ridiculous fluorescent-pink card again. Does she cross out the previous nomination year with a glitter pen and write the current one down? For fuck's sake, is this really what eighteen years in this industry has devolved into—being asked questions from the same type of notecard an eight-year-old girl might study her vocabulary words?

"Cordelia?" hesitantly asked a mid-western accent, interrupting the irritated ruminations of Cordelia Wainwright.

"You know, Patti, I am just happy to be nominated again," Cordelia politely answered.

"Well, you must be the happiest woman in Hollywood, this being your seventh nomination. Will this be lucky number seven?"

This bitch!

Attempting to remain calm, Cordelia answered, "I do not believe in luck or superstitions, Patti. I had enough of that bullshite…oh, dear… Cut! Right, we will do that again.

"I do not believe in luck or superstitions, Patti. The summer I turned twelve, my mother traveled across the UK with the RSC, playing Lady Macbeth—a role she was born to play. I whistled backstage at every dress rehearsal and performance, and never once was she crushed by a sandbag.

"That said, while *Solace Alone* is my seventh overall nomination, it is only my fifth for Best Actress. The other two were for Best Supporting Actress, one of which, as you mentioned, I won."

"Yes, but that was seventeen years ago. Surely—" Patti started.

Nope, not this year, I am over this bullshite!

"Right, let me stop you there, Patti, before you alienate every film actress who has never been nominated for what they thought was the performance of their life. I was fortunate enough to win an Oscar for my very first film. I have made thirty-six since—five, which won Best Picture. My body of work speaks for itself. So, no, I am not sitting at home night after night lovingly stroking my goddamn Oscar like Gollum and calling it 'my precious' in the hopes of completing a set.

"Cut! Can I say 'goddamn' on American broadcast telly? UK censors are more liberal, you see. Just edit that part, if need be, Patti. Next question…"

Smile.

Frazzled by Cordelia's profanity, Patti attempted to refocus the interview. "Yes, well… you have some heavy competition this year. You're up against your BFF and former Best Actress winner Aubrey Taylor."

"Yes."

Just smile when she asks it…

Smirking, Patti asked, "Does it put any strain on your friendship, or is it just a good-old-fashioned 'friendly' rivalry?"

With a plastered smile on her face, Cordelia answered, "Aubrey is a very talented actress, so I am honored to be nominated alongside her again."

"I guess you take some pride in her past win since you were the one who discovered her."

Silence.

"Cordelia?"

"Oh, pardon me. I was not sure if that was a question or just supposition on your part.

"No, I do not take pride in the success of my much-talked-about great 'discovery.' Quite frankly, I find that question not only stupid but offensive, especially since I only 'discovered' Aubrey because Emma Jones got knocked up and had to drop out three months before shooting started on *Nightingales*."

* * *

May 15, 2008: Los Angeles, CA

Cordelia stood off to the side, silently observing the cast and crew of her latest film, *Chimera*. They were drinking champagne and talking amongst themselves about their upcoming projects.

This being her twentieth film and the eleventh as a co-producer, she was used to having to attend these events. She'd smile and pretend to sip champagne, constantly checking her Van Cleef & Arpels watch every few minutes to see if thirty minutes had elapsed. Etiquette demanded that she spend half an hour with the people who tirelessly worked on a movie for which she would make gobs of money—or, so her mother said. But then, not a second after half-past whatever hour, her good-natured but shockingly stupid assistant, Keisha, would appear like a bit too overweight cherub from the heavens to inform everyone that Ms. Wainwright had a call. Then Cordelia would politely excuse herself from the festivities. Not that anyone probably noticed or cared, since no one dared to speak to her at these parties or on set, since it was a very spoken rule that no one should ever start an unsolicited conversation with her.

"Um, would you like a fresh glass of champagne, Ms. Wainwright?" asked a raspy female voice from the side.

Cordelia turned toward the voice and saw a dark-haired young woman, wearing a way too short red skirt, holding two glasses of champagne—one presumably for her.

What is this girl's name? She played the sister of Jonathan... Audra? Aurora?

The girl's fiery light-brown eyes twinkled when she realized Cordelia had no idea who was standing before her. "Um, it's Aubrey. I was in three scenes with you and Jon," she clarified as she pushed a glass of champagne toward Cordelia.

"Yes, right. I was impressed with how well you paced your lines in the courtroom scene." Cordelia took the offered glass and nervously gulped down half of it.

"Really! That means a lot coming from you. Thank you so much!" Aubrey said way too enthusiastically.

Chill out, Aubrey; she's gonna think you're a stalker. Speak normal, not like Jennifer Jason Leigh.

"But, if I'm being completely candid, I sorta drew on your confession scene from *The Honesty of the Law*."

Nope, that was so much fucking worse.

And then something happened that no one had heard once on the fifteen-week shoot of *Chimera*, Cordelia laughed. "Well, I hope your interpretation plays better with the critics. 'Let's be honest folks; Cordelia Wainwright hasn't given an authentic performance since drowning herself in *Hamlet*.'"

Without thinking, Aubrey derisively said, "Who gives a fuck what the critics think, right?"

This elicited a louder laugh from Cordelia. Upon hearing it, a few party-goers wondered if she might be drunk.

"I expect the studios and the audience."

"I'm sorry, I shouldn't—" Aubrey embarrassedly began.

"Don't be. It's refreshing to hear the truth in this hellscape of a town. '*Hell is empty and all the devils are here,*' you know."

"*'But are they, Ariel?'*"Aubrey asked.

Surprise washed over Cordelia's face. "You know *The Tempest*, do you?"

"I did a lot of summer stock in high school."

"Impressive…at least to me. My mother, on the other hand, would have told you that you skipped a few lines," Cordelia said sardonically.

As Aubrey was about to say something she just knew Cordelia would find amusing, a rather nervous-sounding Texas drawl interrupted her.

"Oh, thank goodness I found you, Ms. Wainwright! You have an important call."

Perturbed by the disturbance, Cordelia turned around and shot her plump assistant Keisha the 'not fucking now' look.

"It's a *really* important call, Ma'am," hesitantly said the confused assistant.

Agitated by Keisha's persistence, Cordelia turned back toward Aubrey. "Please excuse her, Aubrey. She was raised by a pack of East Texas wolves, who did not emphasize manners."

Oblivious as always, Keisha corrected her boss. "We don't have wolves in East Texas, Ma'am. We do have coyotes, though."

Cordelia whipped back around so fast that the assistant awkwardly stumbled backward. "Goddammit, Keisha! I do not need a zoological tutorial, nor do I presently need that 'really' important phone call."

Having regained her momentary loss of balance, Keisha stared at Cordelia as though she had no idea what to do or say next. She could see the muscles in Cordelia's jaws tightening and her icy-blue eyes narrowing. She knew if she didn't speak up instantly, there would be a repeat of the time when she accidentally coughed and didn't cover her mouth. She'd been 'sacked,' Ms. Wainwright's word, for three days before Cordelia called and said all was forgiven.

Yeah, right, all was certainly not forgiven! Keisha thought.

First, Cordelia routinely sacked her, but because her boss loathed having new people around, almost more than poor hygiene, she was always rehired within the week. Second, she had to wear a surgical mask for nearly a month afterward, which caused a rash to break out on the bridge of her nose, which caused Cordelia to glare suspiciously at her for another week after that.

"Brenda and Geoffrey are in your dressing room," the words tumbled out almost as quickly as the assistant scurried away to avoid telling Cordelia why.

Oh, this isn't good, Cordelia thought uneasily.

And, then, without so much as a wave back at the young woman she'd been bantering with, she set off for her dressing room, somewhat hearing Aubrey say behind her, "Um, well, it was nice talking to you, Ms. Wainwright."

* * *

Cordelia was standing outside her half-open dressing room door listening to the muffled voices of her agent and lawyer, Brenda Specter, and her long-time producer and business manager, Geoffrey Abbott—or, as she referred to them, *Frick and Frack.* Although she couldn't make out what they were animatedly discussing, she knew that it had to be terribly dreadful because while they would rather be trapped in a room with a rabid dog than with one another, they disliked upsetting her more.

Just one more day…just one more fucking day…

The jabbering stopped when the door swung completely open, and they nervously focused on Cordelia.

"*'Though it be honest, it is never good to bring bad news.'* And every non-Egyptian fiber of my being tells me this is exceptionally terrible news. Right, let's have it, then," Cordelia demanded.

The reluctant bearers of unwelcome news looked at one another, imploring the other to speak first.

Exasperated with their silence, Cordelia threw herself into the makeup chair and slowly started turning in circles like a child might when bored. "Is someone dead?"

"No!" they answered simultaneously.

"Did my husband get arrested for yet another DUI?" Continuous circling.

"No."

"Did Dr. Shapiro cut back my Prozac dosage?" Counterclockwise circling.

"No, nothing like that, CW, but..." Brenda's voice trailed off.

The swiveling chair came to an abrupt halt when Cordelia suddenly stood up. "Just fucking say it, for fuck's sake!"

"There's no easy way to say this—" the producer began.

"Obviously!" Cordelia bellowed.

"You see, Delia, it's about Emma Jones. She's dropping out of *Nightingales*," Geoffrey finished.

"Why?" Cordelia looked at one and then the other for a rational explanation as to why a twenty-five-year-old nobody, whose solitary claim to fame was playing a busty nurse on a glorified nighttime soap, would forgo co-starring in a film with an Oscar-winning actress.

Brenda realized Geoffrey felt he'd dealt the first blow, and it was now her turn to share in the coming ire. "Well, you see, CW, she's pregnant."

"Well, that is easily handled, is it not?" Cordelia coolly asked and turned away from them to look at herself in the dressing mirror.

I might cut my hair at home—perhaps in a lob. It will grow out enough by September...and who will really care, anyway, since I will wear a bonnet most of the time?

"Are you suggesting what I think you're suggesting, CW?" Brenda asked uneasily.

Still peering intently at the length of her strawberry-blond hair, Cordelia gazed back at the usually unflappable agent.

Do not look at me with those judgmental, dead eyes of yours.

Yet, when she saw Brenda purse her lips and ever-so-slightly tilt her chin to the side, Cordelia knew this solution had already been proposed and rejected.

Bloody Hell!

"Can we not just front-load all of her scenes to be shot in September? It is not like this is some elaborate costume film with corsets and cinched waistlines. She will be wearing a fucking shapeless frock and apron most of the time. For fuck's sake, it is not like there really were a bunch of attractive, fit nurses running about Crimea!"

"Come September, she'll be well into her third trimester, Delia, and her obstetrician doesn't think she'd be capable of keeping up with such a…" Geoffrey paused.

"Such a what?" Cordelia demanded, slowly turning back around to look at them.

Frick and Frack—always skating around the truth.

"Perhaps if American actresses ate a bloody sausage roll or steak pie every now and again, instead of subsisting on cocaine and bananas, their bodies would not feel as though the Allies were storming it when another life-form invaded it. I will have you know that my mother did seven shows a week as Desdemona well up into her ninth month. She was smothered by a goddamn pillow night after night and still had a healthy baby—but a twelve-hour workday is too much?"

Geoffrey and Brenda glanced knowingly at one another: *It was always more than twelve hours.*

A shared look of resignation washed over the faces of the ineffectual duo. Both *Frick and Frack* knew that there was no making her see reason now. American vanity and permeability never trumped English humility and durability, *Thus Spoke Cordelia.* They didn't dare mention that her inflexibility in refusing to work in the States in the summer was why she now found herself without a co-star.

What now? Filming is set to begin the first week of September, and I leave for London tomorrow. I am not delaying my holiday to watch auditions. And are there any decent actresses available on such short notice? If I leave it to Geoffrey, I will spend three-and-a-half months working alongside whatever slag he is currently shagging.

"You two," Cordelia forcefully pointed her French-manicured index finger at them while stalking toward the still-open dressing-room door, "follow me!"

As she marched down the dimly lit hallway, she could hear raised voices and loud music coming from the party. She knew the lure of free liquor alone guaranteed more than a few potential candidates.

Her unexpected reemergence was met by bewildered faces, and someone hurried to turn down Katy Perry's "I Kissed a Girl." Cordelia paid no mind as she coolly and clinically surveyed the room.

Too old. She bathes in perfume! Too blond. Too slaggy—that is probably why she is always late! Too plain. Too chatty. Too tall. That one is constantly sneezing! Too ambitious. Ah, there she is—pretty, but not too pretty; dark-haired; thin, but not anorexic; very nice legs; and, her smile is goofy enough to pass for English.

With two finger snaps, Cordelia summoned *Frick and Frack* to her side and pointed at Aubrey. "Bring me that one, and do not fucking tell her why."

* * *

They found her hunched over and scribbling into a Letts' planner. If Cordelia heard them come in, she didn't acknowledge it. The only audible sound was the soft whirling vibration created by the nib of her Conway Stewart fountain pen etching words across a page.

Aubrey knew the room served as both an office and dressing room for the star whenever she was filming at Willowbrook, the production company Cordelia and Geoffrey started in 2003, so she was surprised to find nothing to distract her from her ever-growing anxiety about being summoned.

All four walls were white and bare, with no movie posters or cast photos anywhere. There were no pictures of any kind. The makeup on the dressing table was neatly stacked, and the closet was empty. There was, however, an open jar of black ink and what appeared to be a pair of circa 1990 spongy headphones wrapped around a Walkman CD player sitting atop the small desk Cordelia was furiously writing at.

With nothing to draw her attention away from the uncomfortable position Aubrey now found herself in, the babbling dam broke.

"Do you think Bartleby would have *preferred* to listen to Beyoncé or Oasis while scrivening?"

Without looking up, Cordelia answered behind a smile, "He strikes me as more of a The Cure sort of bloke," and continued, well, scrivening.

Brenda and Geoffrey gave one another side-eyed glances that fell somewhere between horror and bemusement, while Aubrey nervously clasped her hands tightly behind her back, slowly bobbing her head, and flexing her knees.

"I hear Bupropion is an adequate solution for that." Cordelia smirked as she straightened upright in her chair, capped her pen, and tightened the ink jar lid. "You are obviously well-read. Where did you go to uni?"

Unnecessarily, Brenda translated, "She's asking where you went to college."

"Um, yeah…I studied theater at Dartmouth."

"That's in New Hampshire, CW," said the once-translator turned geographer.

"Do you have any upcoming projects in the works?" Cordelia asked.

"I have a few auditions lined up, but—"

"What are the chances you will be with child in September?" Cordelia cut her off before she could continue with the struggling actress's lament.

"Don't answer that!" Brenda interjected, remembering that she was a lawyer. "We've been over this, CW. Does Keisha watch those HR videos for you?"

A slight groan emanated from Cordelia's throat.

Why are Americans so litigious?

And yet, while Americans certainly loved suing one another, penniless actresses sharing two-bedroom apartments in the Valley with three other penniless actresses were exceptionally fond of eating and paying their rent.

"I'm gay, so unless I'm touched by an angel in the next three months, I don't think that's gonna be an issue."

Both of Cordelia's hands came together in a solitary thundering clap. "Perfect! Can you do an English accent?"

Almost simultaneously, Aubrey's face, neck, and ears turned the deepest shade of crimson ever captured on the color spectrum, and an exasperated Brenda shouted, "Goddammit, CW!"

Truly unaware that she'd violated several harassment statutes, which Keisha had learned about in the production company's HR videos, and fully mistaking Aubrey's apparent embarrassment, Cordelia obliviously continued, "There is no need to get all bothered if you do not. We can tutor you."

Silent up to this moment, Geoffrey stepped in before Brenda had a stroke. "That's a grand idea, Delia. I'll call Peg Sharpe straight away and see if she's available to be Aubrey's *dialect* coach."

Brenda shook her head in defeat and mouthed 'thank you' to the ultimate translator of Cordelia Wainwright.

Is it a British thing?

"Right, well, now what shall we do about Anton? He had his cap set on 'directing' Emma. Do you think he is the father? Oh… but if he were, he would probably know that she is out…"

"He's literally been neutered, so no," Brenda clarified Cordelia's wandering thoughts.

With her skin having resumed its typical shade of California tan and her heart rate back to something resembling stable, Aubrey came to a life-altering realization: this wasn't just some bit part but a co-starring role in a Willowbrook production.

"Just so we're clear—I had about five glasses of champagne at the party—are you offering me Emma Jones' role in *Nightingales?*"

"I do not know, Aubrey." Cordelia stood, unwound the wires of the dated headphones from the Walkman and then put them around her neck. She then gathered up her embossed planner, placed the CD player atop it, and tucked both under her left arm. She took three long strides towards the young actress, which landed them face-to-face. "Are you a Bartleby or a Pompey? For it is said, '*Who seeks, and will not take when once 'tis offered, shall never find it more.*'"

Aubrey's light-brown eyes mischievously flickered. "You know he ends up murdered, right?"

Feeling challenged by the young actress's impertinence, Cordelia took her right index finger and thumb to tilt Aubrey's chin upward. She moved it slowly from side to side, never taking her penetrating ice-blue gaze from Aubrey's own. She leaned in so close that Aubrey could feel the star's breath on her tingling skin, and Brenda could feel a lawsuit coming on, and said, barely above a whisper, "Yes, but would you rather starve to death alone or be killed for taking a chance at glory?"

When Aubrey didn't answer with a smart-ass remark, Cordelia took a step back and grinned in a self-satisfied way as she struggled to put the headphones on with one hand. "Shooting begins September 2nd—and, by the way, I *prefer* The Cure."

As she made her way out the door, she yelled over her shoulder to *Frick and Frack*, "You are welcome. And do not bloody fucking ring me!"

* * *

Sept. 19, 2008: Los Angeles, CA

"Cut! For fuck's sake, stop bloody fidgeting! Do you have some sort of neurological disorder, or have you forgotten to take your Bupropion again?"

What response was there to give to yet another tyrannical, irrational, and scornful outburst? For three very long weeks, Aubrey had endured this never-ending barrage of insults. Each time, and there were countless, Aubrey and every member of the cast and crew just stared at each other dumbfounded.

Yes, everyone knew that *she* could be difficult and demanding—most of them had worked with *her* more times than they wished to remember—but this was a whole new side of Cordelia Wainwright. A very dark, bitter side. The collective consensus was that *she* was in the throes of a complete mental breakdown. Most were surprised that it had taken so long.

Worse, they were behind schedule, which only exacerbated the production from hell. She despised being behind schedule almost more than anything—so much more than even tardiness, sloppiness, nosiness, and/or chattiness.

"Perhaps we should take a *short* break, Delia," Geoffrey gently suggested to the temperamental star as he emerged from the shadows behind the lights.

"No more fucking breaks, Geoffrey!" she shouted and stomped her right foot down so forcefully to the ground that Geoffrey knew that it was absolutely time for a break.

"Right…so everyone, we'll take lunch and then reconvene…" *How long does it take to commit someone again?* "About one o'clock."

No one needed to be told twice, and they all scurried away like rats off a fully ablaze, sinking ship.

When the set was clear, Geoffrey and Cordelia stood silently watching the other, waiting to see who would speak first. But what could be said that hadn't already been said—ad nauseam?

Frustrated, Cordelia threw her hands up, curtly spun around on her heels, and stormed away.

Geoffrey just watched her in a somewhat defeated way and then heard it echo down the hallway: "Goddammit to bloody fucking hell!" And, for good measure, as if she hadn't expressed her anger quite thoroughly enough, she slammed her dressing room door shut so hard that he wondered if she might have finally wrecked the door frame beyond repair.

* * *

After waiting the standard *CCP—Cordelia Cool-down Period*, at least fifteen minutes—he entered the dressing room to find her crumpled over her desk, face-down with her hands tightly crossed over her head like a child serving a timeout at recess.

Hmmmmmmmmmmmmmmmm…

He walked lightly toward the makeup chair, lest he disturb the petulant child, sat down, and gingerly swiveled his seat to face her tiny black desk. He contemplated his next move as he slowly ran his hands down the length of his gray Savile Row trousers. He'd known her all of her life and, more importantly, since the start of her acting career. He was well acquainted with the temper tantrums and pouting.

Her parents, Beatrice and Henry, had been his friends since the late-1970s when he first began his producing career in London's West End theater district. For over 150 years, the Wainwright family had been putting on Shakespearean productions in Mayfair. Every generation was expected to work, in some capacity, at the Wainwright Theater.

Cordelia was an acutely awkward child who rarely spoke and shied away from the spotlight. As such, she'd had no desire to become an actress. Her mother, however, would have none of it. She may have accepted it if her oldest daughter had been unattractive or cursed with an unpleasant voice. But Cordelia was a beautiful young woman with wavy, strawberry-blond hair, striking ice-blue eyes, and *passable* elocution. Once her secondary education was complete at age sixteen, she did her further education studies at the Wainwright, with her mother as head tutor. This did not go well for either mother or daughter—and it was also when the tantrums began.

"Perchance, did something happen over your holiday…at *home*?" Geoffrey started.

Silence.

"No dust-ups of any kind, then?"

Silence.

"So, everything is the same as…*always*?" Geoffrey finally asked, knowing this would draw a reaction.

"Don't analyze me, Geoffrey." When she sat up, there were tear streaks, and her puffy eyes were bloodshot. "I do not know if I can do *this* anymore."

That's new…Not the words but the tears. The only time Cordelia wept was on cue, so Geoffrey's level of concern immediately went from moderate to critical. He glanced down at his gold Rolex and frowned as imperceptibly as he could.

"Right, well, I'll give you a moment to collect your…thoughts, and then we'll have a good chat."

As he hastily retreated, Cordelia collapsed dejectedly onto the desk and began mentally preparing for what she knew was coming next.

Thirty minutes later, she heard the door open, and without lifting her head from the desk, she held out her right hand. Geoffrey handed her his phone and wordlessly shut the door.

When Cordelia didn't issue a salutation to the party on the other end, she was greeted with, "I can hear you pouting over 8,000 kilometers away, Darling."

Silence.

"The headmaster says that you are not playing well with the other children at school. Care to explain why?" asked Beatrice Wainwright's stern but not unkind voice.

"I want to come home, Mother. I am...lonely." She sounded so pitifully pathetic.

"Then come home, Darling."

This was not the first, nor the hundredth time, that either this call or this simple statement of fact been made. Every time, just as now, Cordelia said, "You know very well that I cannot."

"Nonsense! I know no such thing, Delia," Beatrice's voice turned a touch sharper. "I do *know* that a twenty-eight-year-old woman does not throw temper tantrums and eviscerate young actresses in front of her colleagues for fidgeting *just* because she's homesick."

Silence.

"Geoffrey says that the poor girl isn't even that bad of an actress, for Hollywood, but that you constantly find fault with her, which only worsens her fluttering hands. Perhaps if you were more encouraging and, dare I say, *friendly* toward her, then you could right the ship."

Silence.

"Right, so this is what you *will* do...are you listening to me?" Beatrice demanded.

"Yes, Mother."

"First, you are going to stop being so beastly to this girl, *at once*, and apologize—no, it does not have to be in front of anyone. God forbid! And then you'll make nice and invite her to dinner at that sterile laboratory you call a house."

"But, Mother..." Cordelia stammered.

"No buts, Delia! I will ring Mrs. Holt myself to let her know that you and Bradley—assuming he's anywhere around—will have a dinner guest tomorrow. Am I understood?"

Cordelia knew it was pointless to argue. "Yes, Mother."

"Good! Mummy loves you gobs, but this session has made me late for the theater."

* * *

When filming resumed at one o'clock, Cordelia was eerily normal—*for her*. There were no more preemptive *Cuts!* or livid outbursts. When Aubrey did something that displeased her, which was often—namely moving her head too much or flexing her hands when she shouldn't—*one flex, double flex, shake out, and repeat*—Cordelia waited for Anton, the director, to say something. It helped that she'd taken an extra Prozac and Valium after her 'Phone a Mother Lifeline.' She floated through the rest of the day as though nothing had happened, and no one mentioned that her icy-blue eyes were more dilated than usual.

After shooting wrapped for the day, Aubrey went to her dressing room to quickly change out of her long-sleeved, gray tweed nurse costume. She had plans to go clubbing with her roommates that evening and was late, as usual, because filming had run two hours past schedule. As she was going out the door, she came face-to-face with Keisha.

"Ms. Wainwright would like to see you." Nothing more needed to be said, and the assistant returned down the hallway.

I'm definitely getting fired, Aubrey thought.

When she arrived at Cordelia's door, it was open—it was never open.

"Um, Ms. Wainwright, you wanted to see me?" Aubrey hesitantly asked.

Just as it had been on her first summoning, Cordelia was seated, head down, at her desk scribbling. She didn't look up to acknowledge Aubrey but instead waved her left hand to indicate that Aubrey was permitted to enter.

There Aubrey stood silently for two very long minutes, trying her best not to fidget or say anything clever—or stupid. It was a struggle. No seat was offered, not that there was one to be proffered other than Cordelia's makeup chair. Apparently, the star didn't have many visitors.

Much to the relief of Aubrey's ever-growing concern about how she would pay her bills, Cordelia finally stopped writing and looked up.

Is this what she is spending her wages on?

Before Cordelia stood a tense twenty-three-year-old woman wearing a form-fitting short red Balenciaga dress with a slit running straight up the left hip.

Exactly how much is Geoffrey paying her?

"I had Keisha look you up on IMDb. This is your third film, correct?" It was said more as a statement and less than as a question.

"Um, yes, Ms. Wainwright." *I hope it's not the last.*

"I recall you mentioning that you studied theater at Dartmouth, correct?" Again, more statement, less question.

"Um, yes, Ms. Wainwright."

"Right, well, stage acting and film acting are not the same—"

"Am I getting fired?" Aubrey impertinently blurted out. *One flex, double flex, shake out and repeat.*

Her outburst startled Cordelia, who was not accustomed to being interrupted while speaking.

If only that were possible.

"No, of course not. It is just that, well, you have some... mechanics that are more suited to stage acting. In theater, it is perfectly well and good to...exaggerate your movements—such as moving your head and hands about to communicate to the audience. Film acting is more nuanced and still—less about body motion."

"Yes, I understand, Ms. Wainwright. I'll try to work on that." Aubrey was relieved she could continue paying her rent.

Must I really do this?

It took every ounce of Cordelia's considerable acting skill to smile when she began her version of an apology. "I expect you are a bit overwhelmed, this being your first significant role, so nervousness is completely normal. I may have been a bit... hasty, dropping you into it without more consideration." *Bloody Hell!* "And, so...I think you should come to the house for dinner tomorrow, and afterward, I will tutor you on how to use your body more effectively."

Aubrey sucked her lips in tightly to stop from giggling like a teenager. Along with the direct insults, she'd also gotten used to Cordelia's malapropisms.

Why is she chewing her lips? Is this yet another affliction?

"Right, well, no need to dress up," Cordelia said, slowly scanning Aubrey's outfit, which revealed way too much leg. "Casual will do. I will have Keisha text you the details."

She then returned to the papers on her desk, which was Aubrey's signal that she was dismissed. Aubrey didn't take the hint.

"Um, why don't you use a regular pen—wouldn't it be less... *messy?*"

Without looking up, Cordelia smirked. "Contrary to popular belief, I sometimes *prefer* messy things. Good night, Ms. Taylor."

CHAPTER TWO

"The Temptress"

Sept. 20, 2008: Irvine, CA

The house was in a gated community in Irvine. When Aubrey drove her 2003 red Volkswagen Beetle to the end of the long driveway, she was surprised to find a modestly sized ranch-style cornflower blue-brick home. This was not your typical, over-the-top movie star mansion.

Before she could ring the bell, the door swung open, and a tall, muscular man in his early forties with sandy-blond hair, wearing khaki cargo shorts and a blue button-down shirt, greeted her.

"Welcome, Aubrey! I hope you didn't have any problem with the gate."

"Um, no..." Aubrey mumbled.

No introductions were needed. Aubrey had been in Hollywood for nearly two years and met her fair share of stars, but she'd never encountered one quite as famous as Bradley Simpson, Cordelia's husband of five years. His *Lycan* franchise was worth billions.

They obviously didn't spend it on this place, Aubrey thought.

"Come on in! CWs in the kitchen helping Mrs. H finish up the grub. You can put your shoes by the door." Bradley pointed at a clear plastic mat inside the entrance.

While the outside may have been unimposing, the inside of the house was overwhelmingly and immaculately white. The walls, the Italian marble floors, the bookshelves, the Wynn leather couch, and the marble oversized square-shaped coffee table were *so, so, so white*. Although Aubrey knew the couple were childless, one look at this décor would have confirmed it to anyone unaware.

"Do you think she'll let us eat in here?" Bradley joked, seeing Aubrey's eyes working their way around the living room.

She chuckled but didn't have time to respond because Cordelia suddenly appeared out of the dining room dressed in tailored black Barbour trousers and a pink satin short-sleeved blouse.

"Hello, I see you found us."

"Um, yeah. You have a lovely home, Ms. Wainwright." *More like a museum.*

Her only response was an almost indiscernible smile. "Dinner is ready in the *dining room*," Cordelia announced, with a backward glance aimed directly at Bradley.

The dining room was identical to the living room—white, *so, so, so white*.

Dinner consisted of beef Wellington, parsnips, cauliflower, a raspberry trifle, and milk or water to drink—Cordelia didn't consume alcohol if she could avoid it. The china was Wedgwood, the cutlery Arthur Price, and the crystal Royal Brierley. Had Aubrey known the collective cost of what she was dragging her fork across, incorrectly cutting her meat with, and drinking her water from, she might have been much gentler when she scraped the cream around and out of her trifle cup. Cordelia did her best not to cringe.

The conversation was sparse and conducted, primarily one-sided, by Bradley, who was gearing up for a location shoot of *Lycan Unleashed* in Budapest. For twenty minutes, in between bites, he rambled on about how excited he was to go to various castles and the Hungarian Opera House to watch Puccini's *La bohème*.

From time to time, Aubrey would hear Cordelia say, "Sounds delightful…" and then return to silently eating her English food.

"So, Aubrey, what's it like working with old CW?"

The question was jarring. First, it came out of nowhere as Bradley's animated personal tour of Hungary abruptly halted. Second, Aubrey wanted to remain employed.

Bradley's sudden inquiry into work relations at Willowbrook drew a sharp head turn from his wife and a clenched jaw and thinning lips.

"She talks about you *all* the time," Bradley continued, ignoring Cordelia's glare.

"I bet," Aubrey sarcastically retorted.

"Right, so it looks like everyone is finished. Shall we go into the other room so Mrs. Holt can clear." Cordelia stood up and dropped her linen napkin on the table.

Dinner was over.

* * *

Once settled in the living room, Bradley went to one of the bookshelves and opened a door that served as his hidden liquor cabinet.

"What's your poison, Aubrey?"

An audible sound of severe dissatisfaction from Cordelia was heard by all. She avoided hard liquor, and he knew it. She found its effects on him particularly distasteful—he'd had three DUIs in their five-year marriage.

"What…I'm home. It's not like I'm driving," Bradley bargained with his wife.

"Yes, but *she* is," Cordelia snapped at him, looking toward Aubrey, who was awkwardly and uncomfortably sitting on the edge of the last white cushion of the couch.

"One drink won't make her run off the road, CW. You look like a tequila girl, Aubrey."

Cordelia could see Aubrey wanted to say yes but was too afraid to do so. "Fine, *one* drink…and not like you would pour yourself—and mix it with something."

"Do you know how to make a Ranch Water?" Aubrey asked, thankful that Cordelia had acquiesced to her husband's request. *God, I need it.*

"1800, lime juice, and Topo Chico coming right up."

Once the drinks were dispensed, it was time to get down to brass tacks.

"So, we might start by working on your launch stance. You have a habit of shifting your feet." Cordelia stood and, by her stare, indicated that Aubrey should do the same.

As Aubrey was about to place her half-empty glass on the coffee table without a coaster, Bradley whisked the glass from her hand and half-whispered, "We wouldn't want you to get off on the wrong foot with your tutor."

Ignoring her husband's jab, Cordelia continued with the lesson.

"A good actress keeps her feet firmly planted on the ground, her head up, her shoulders back, and her knees slightly bent. In most circumstances, your feet and torso should be pointed directly at the camera. So, pretend that Bradley is the camera and assume the correct position."

"Just what kind of film are you planning on making, CW?" Bradley lewdly asked, which made Aubrey laugh.

"The kind where CGI does not do all the heavy lifting," Cordelia caustically replied.

"Ouch! Someone's more irritable than usual." Bradley leaned back too quickly on the couch, precariously juggling the two glasses in his hands.

"Goddammit, Bradley! If you stain my fucking couch, it will be *you* and *not* Mrs. Holt who will be steam-cleaning it!"

Assured that her pristine couch was safe from his clumsiness, Cordelia took a moment to compose herself and then motioned for Aubrey to stand in front of Bradley. Once her pupil was in the proper stance, Cordelia walked behind her and put her hands on Aubrey's hips. This unnerved Aubrey.

"Now, this is a nice, static stance. When we want to move our head, we do it with evenness, either up or down." Cordelia brought her right hand up to Aubrey's chin, softly gripped it with her thumb and index finger, and performed the motion for her. "Or right to left, as such," again, performing the motion for her. "Now, you do it."

As Aubrey mimicked the motion, she couldn't help but look at Bradley, who was watching this lesson intently. He didn't look licentious but curious—as though he were dissecting and cataloging his findings.

"Good!" Cordelia said from behind her, snapping Aubrey's focus back to the task at hand.

"Now, we will work on your hand and arm movements. Arms are difficult because they just hang, but thankfully, we have hands to guide them. Our hands and arms convey nonverbal messages, so how you use them tells part of your character...Sarah's story.

"She is not a fidgety Hollywood actress but a young nurse not prone to histrionics. So, when she wipes the tears from her face in *Scene XIII*, she does it as such..." Cordelia cupped Aubrey's right arm with her own, put her hand flat under Aubrey's, then slowly brought it up to Aubrey's face and gently wiped away an imaginary tear.

And then Aubrey and Bradley saw them: goosebumps up and down Cordelia's right arm. Aubrey was startled—*No fucking way!*—and looked at Bradley, who knowingly grinned at her and tapped the tip of his nose four times with his index finger.

"I think that's enough tutoring for tonight, CW. It's Aubrey's night off, after all."

"Right, well, that's probably a good idea..." Cordelia was clearly flushed. She hastily dropped Aubrey's arm and immediately crossed her own against her chest to hide the evidence.

Cordelia's irrational, childish behavior towards her on set made more sense to Aubrey now: *She's blushing...this crazy bitch is into me!*

The pure, unmitigated shock on Aubrey's face was enough to tell Bradley that she finally got it. He stood up and announced, "I have an early workout in the morning, so I'm gonna head off to *my* bed after I drop these glasses in the kitchen." When he was nearly out of the room, he swung back around. "Have you ever seen an Oscar up close and personal, Aubrey?"

"Um, no…"

"She doesn't want to see that silly thing, Bradley," Cordelia said as steadily as she could manage.

What the fuck are you doing—Sunday is the only fucking day of the week that you don't work out at that bloody gym!

"Sure she does—what actress wouldn't? You practically sleep with yours. She keeps it in *her* bedroom, Aubrey, so it's the first thing she sees when she wakes up and the last thing at night. Goodnight, ladies!"

There was a long, awkward silence after he left, which was broken by Cordelia saying, "Right, well, it's getting late, so I expect it's time for you to go, too. You probably have a long drive back, and who knows what the 405 will be like."

Aubrey should have known better, but she couldn't resist the temptation to find out. "I'd like to see it…your Oscar, if you don't mind."

I do bloody mind!

"Right, well, then, follow me."

* * *

"There it is," Cordelia swept her right hand toward a wall-length walnut bookcase, where her Best Supporting Actress statue stood perfectly centered.

This room was not like the rest of the house—*so, so, so white*. It looked like a human lived in it.

The walls were soft lavender, and all the furniture, except a black, gold-inlaid pigeonhole desk, was made of warm walnut wood. And, then, there was the bookcase. Aubrey, of course, was impressed by the 13 ½ inch tall gold man sitting directly in the center of it, but the sheer number of photographs of Cordelia's family drew her focus.

Cordelia sensed Aubrey's fascination with the pictures, walked over to one of her favorites, and took it off the bookcase. "This is my mother, Beatrice, and my sisters Miranda and Portia, and this is Ophy," she said, identifying each person in the photo with her index finger.

"You all look so…alike," Aubrey said.

"Yes, well, we're all Wainwrights, you see," Cordelia joked. "Right, well, so you've seen Oscar, so now, I think—"

Realizing she was about to be shown the door, Aubrey interrupted, "Why doesn't Bradley sleep in here?"

"I expect he sheds, an occupational hazard I—"

But, before she could finish whatever British witticism she planned to say, Aubrey roughly grabbed Cordelia's face with both hands and kissed her. It only lasted a few seconds before Cordelia frantically pushed her away and clumsily backed into the black desk.

"What…this is highly…unprofessional! I'm your superior…" Cordelia was clearly flustered, bothered, confused, and many other adverbs as she ran her hand anxiously through her strawberry-blond hair.

"I know that you like me—like, you *really, really, really* like me," Aubrey said, slowly closing the distance between them.

Good God, what is the girl doing?

"I've no idea what you're referring to, but clearly there has been some…"

Before she could continue with her protestations, though, Aubrey stood uncomfortably close, peering directly into her icy-blue eyes—waiting. What could Cordelia say? Her skin tingled, and she could feel the tiny hairs on her arms and neck standing on end. She knew she could speak, but she couldn't say…anything. Worse, her mouth felt like it was full of cotton, and her lips were as dry as the Mojave.

When Cordelia nervously licked her lips for the much-needed moisture, Aubrey took one step closer, took Cordelia's face into her hands, and rasped, "I *know* from the look in those beautiful blue eyes of yours that you want me. Please kiss me, Cordy."

Cordelia stared at Aubrey's full, pouty lips, leaned into them, and did as directed. At first, she kissed the object of her desire slowly and softly but then more deeply and passionately. It was a scene she'd played numerous times in her films: the romantic, passionate kiss that finally resolved the couple's sexual tension.

Yet, this time, she didn't feel an instant need to disinfect her mouth with Listerine.

I quite like this.

"So, that's why you pulled my pigtails so hard," Aubrey said breathlessly, removing her lips from Cordelia's and sliding them down her swan-like neck.

Cordelia had no idea what that meant, nor did she care, because she could only concentrate on how her body reacted to Aubrey's lips and roving hands. She'd never experienced anything close to it in her twenty-eight years. Usually, having someone smashed up against her body, as Aubrey was now, would have made her nauseous, but Cordelia felt as though she could not pull Aubrey close enough.

When Aubrey's hand drifted underneath Cordelia's pink satin blouse and started gently caressing her breasts, she felt as if every nerve ending in her body were on fire.

"You *really* do like me," Aubrey raspily whispered into Cordelia's ear as she felt a stiff nipple underneath the bra's lace. Aubrey's other hand slowly drifted downward across Cordelia's stomach and stopped just at the waistband of her trousers, hovering. "How much do you *like* me, Cordy?"

"*Desperately…*"

How she said it was guttural and, well, *desperate*, which Aubrey quickly understood because when she put her hand between Cordelia's legs, she was literally drenched with desire.

"My goodness, you *realllllllllllly* like me." Aubrey slid two fingers inside of Cordelia and watched as every successive stroke brought this frigid, uptight germaphobe closer to climax—it didn't take long.

When she came, she practically collapsed on top of Aubrey with relief and thanked her, much to Aubrey's delight and shock, and then she held herself close to Aubrey for several moments, trying to recover both her senses and breathing.

Once she regained her composure, she stood back from Aubrey. "I have never been with a woman—and, if I am being completely honest, I have limited experience when it comes to men as well—but if you…" the words just wouldn't fall out of her mouth.

An enormous smile fully encompassed Aubrey's face. "Would you like me to teach you how?"

"Yes, I would *prefer* that," Cordelia said bashfully, trying her best not to blush.

"First lesson: we take off all of our clothes."

* * *

Sept. 21, 2008: Irvine, CA

Sometime past eight the following morning, Aubrey woke up and extended her arm across the softest cotton sheets she'd ever slept on, *at least 800 thread count*, to find emptiness.

Groggily, she sat up in the queen-sized bed to look for the woman who had clung to her like a kindergartener on her first day at school and begged her not to leave when she'd tried to go home late at night. Cordelia was absent for her second day of school. All Aubrey could do was shake her head and recount what had transpired the night before.

If she were grading her pupil's performance, she would've given Cordelia high marks for effort and written 'Needs Improvement' for execution. She was pretty skilled, if somewhat awkward at the same time, with her hand mechanics, but her oral skills were severally lacking. Aubrey couldn't help but feel sorry for poor Bradley, not necessarily because she was the one currently sitting in his wife's bed, but because it was profoundly evident that he didn't get many blow-jobs.

After she'd modeled the intricacies of cunnilingus on her enthusiastic, to say the very least, student—Cordelia's body had fully convulsed, and she'd literally and irreverently shouted at the top of her lungs, 'Christ Almighty!' when she orgasmed—Aubrey suggested that it was Cordelia's turn to reciprocate in kind, she'd made what could only be described as a grimace. But she tried, be it halfheartedly, to demonstrate what she'd just learned. It was not a successful demonstration by any stretch of the imagination, which Aubrey attributed to Cordelia's lack of experience and complete abhorrence of germs.

As she scanned the bedroom floor for her hastily discarded Levi's and oversized Ralph Lauren red button-down shirt, she found that they, like Cordelia, were nowhere to be seen. Since she had no inkling of when, *if ever*, Cordelia would return to tell her where she'd undoubtedly neatly folded her clothes, Aubrey had no other recourse but to look for something to put on.

As she surveyed Cordelia's walk-in closet of black, tailored everything, sans the occasional white or pink satin or silk blouse, she realized she would have to rummage through Cordelia's chest drawers. She made sure not to disrupt the precisely folded clothes as she searched for something to wear. Much to her relief, she found a pair of draw-string sweatpants—miraculously, gray in color—and a black The Cure T-shirt.

Once fully clothed, she strolled around the bedroom to understand who the woman she'd spent the night with *really* was. Not surprisingly, everything, besides the bedsheets, was tidily placed just so.

A lavender, antique water pitcher and bowl sat atop the chest— without a speck of dust. The dresser was adorned with a neatly arranged assortment of Estée Lauder cosmetics and Burberry perfumes, a tortoiseshell soft-bristled brush and matching comb, Cordelia's platinum wedding band, and a platinum Van Cleef & Arpels watch.

At the black, gold-inlaid pigeonhole desk, Aubrey found that *silly* black Conway Stewart fountain pen Cordelia always wrote with lying perfectly perpendicular in the middle of her Letts' planner. Looking above the desk, she saw a gold-framed reproduction of John Everett Millais' *Ophelia* staring down at her. Aubrey found the painting both creepy and depressing.

Who would want to wake up every morning to see a drowned woman?

And then there was the bookcase, filled with so many gold-framed pictures of Cordelia's family. Aubrey counted at least twenty. The one shelf not filled with photographs and her Oscar contained audiobooks of what appeared to be Cordelia's research material for various film roles. Aubrey couldn't help but think it wasn't a The Cure CD she'd had in that *ridiculous* Walkman of hers that first day in her office, but instead an audio recording of Nicolas Soames' biography of Florence Nightingale.

After waiting an insufferable amount of time for Cordelia to return, Aubrey concluded that she'd have to venture outside the bedroom to find her lost lover—and her missing clothes.

The *so, so, so white* living and dining rooms were vacant, so Aubrey walked into the kitchen, where she found Bradley sitting at an island scarfing down an enormously large bowl of Fruity Pebbles.

"Don't judge me; it's my *cheat* day," he joked. "There's coffee over there if you want some," he indicated with a head nod.

While Aubrey poured herself a cup, she glanced at him, trying to gauge how awkward the situation could get. He certainly didn't come off as a jealous, cuckolded husband—especially since he'd practically tucked her into his wife's bed himself the night before.

"Um, have you seen Cordelia?" she nonchalantly asked.

"Well, she's not at church since apparently she did all her praying last night," he snorted.

Aubrey's face instantly burned red. "So, you heard *that*?"

He could see that the young woman, wearing his wife's clothes, was clearly embarrassed by her walk of shame, and so he decided to go easy on her.

"Here's the thing about CW and me: we're married, but *not* married. She's my beard, and I'm her Green Card... and, now apparently, her beard, too."

"No, fucking way! Lucien the Lycan is gay?" Aubrey was floored.

"For a lesbian, you don't have very good gaydar, do you," he wisecracked. "Yes, but there isn't a huge market out there for queer superheroes—the action figures and video games wouldn't sell well in the Red States—and so Brenda—you've met the Dragonlady, right—hooked up her two misfittiest clients. It works for both of us. I get to have a smoking hot British wife, and she gets to not have to explain to the world just how fucking repressed she is."

"Um, yeah…so does that mean…" Aubrey didn't know how to ask what she was thinking.

"No, she isn't…or wasn't, a virgin before last night. When we first got together, CW told me she'd fucked some dude when she was a teenager but didn't like it and that she was quite happy handling her own needs, if you get my drift. But, I'm pretty sure her come to Jesus moment last night was the first time she'd had someone else get her off, so you can take credit for that one." He held up his right hand for a high-five.

"Do you know where she's at?" Aubrey asked, declining to partake in his frat-boy activity.

"The laundry room—I hope you like starch," he quipped. "By the front door, to the left."

* * *

"There you are," Aubrey said as she opened the laundry room door.

Yes, there she was—wearing a long, black silk robe, standing over a board ironing Aubrey's Levi's, holding, well, a can of Faultless Starch.

"Good morning. I will have your trousers finished soon. There is coffee in the kitchen if you want some," Cordelia said matter-of-factly, barely looking up from the task at hand.

"Yeah, your *husband* showed me where it was," Aubrey dryly quipped as she entered the room and walked over to Cordelia, who was still vigorously creasing her jeans.

Who irons jeans?

Cordelia's head jerked up. "Hmm…right, I surmise by your tone that he explained our…situation?"

"Yep—he fucks dudes, and you masturbate—which explains *a lot*," Aubrey joked and tried to kiss Cordelia, who averted her just a little too fast for Aubrey's liking. "Hey, that's not very friendly!"

Seeing the hurt look on Aubrey's face, she explained, "I do not mean to rebuff you, but, well, I expect you have not yet brushed your teeth this morning."

With a wicked smile, Aubrey said, "I used yours," and tried for another kiss. But, when Cordelia looked as though she might vomit, Aubrey quickly confessed, "I'm joking, Cordy. I used my finger—I swear!"

Cordelia wasn't sure she believed her, but nonetheless gently brushed her lips against Aubrey's pouty ones.

"No one has ever called me Cordy before. I think I quite like the way it sounds."

This admission made Aubrey's heart skip a beat.

It's not like I could keep calling you Ms. Wainwright after last night.

"Do you? So, if I were to say, 'Cordy, you look super sexy in that robe. Please, *Cordy*, please, come back to bed so I can rip it off you,' you would like the sound of that?"

"Very much…as long as you swear you did not use my toothbrush."

CHAPTER THREE

"The Taming of Ms. Wainwright"

Sept. 23, 2008—Dec. 17, 2009: Irvine, CA

Nature is cyclical. One season follows the next, and then, voilà, the universe hits the repeat button and begins anew. Their fifteen-month-long relationship mimicked this same pattern—with a few minor alterations.

In the fall, Cordelia left for the studio at 5:30 a.m. and never returned home before 7:00 p.m.—even after they started sleeping together. On Tuesdays and Thursdays, Aubrey would invite herself over to spend the night and then drive separately back to the lot the following morning.

On the set of *Nightingales*, Cordelia was friendly but never familiar. No knowing glances were passed, and they never found themselves alone. Most weekends consisted of watching documentaries about genocide, disease, and/or pestilence; eating sausage rolls and/or various English meat pies and puddings; and, then, somewhat miraculously, considering their other activities, an indecent amount of sex.

Cordelia had approached her dearth of sexual knowledge as though she were doing research for one of her film roles. This also brought her into the twenty-first century; since she couldn't send Keisha to Barnes & Noble to buy an audiobook on lesbian sex without arousing suspicion—even her clueless assistant was smart enough to put two and two together—Cordelia replaced her dated headphones and CDs with ear buds and pod-casts. She was a dedicated student who thoroughly mastered the subject in a matter of weeks.

Aubrey was extremely satisfied, and Cordelia was somewhat content.

Once winter arrived, however, so did Cordelia's coolness.

Nightingales had wrapped, and Aubrey was auditioning for parts; Cordelia was preparing for her next role in the aptly titled *The Mountain Between Us*; and, so, their Tuesday/Thursday trysts became almost non-existent.

Then there were the weekends, which Aubrey categorized as *BC* and *AD—Before Christmas* and *Always Depressed*.

The first two weekends in December, Cordelia spent mostly on Amazon and very little on, below, underneath, or between Aubrey. Their first Christmastime was spent separately—Cordelia in England and Aubrey in Vermont—with no gifts or phone calls exchanged.

The second week of January brought Cordelia gloomily back to Los Angeles. Although she would never admit it to herself, God forbid Aubrey, she was homesick the second she left her family in London. To cope, her workday schedule somehow became even more grueling, and weekends were spent sleeping—*a lot*. There was no mention of the Big O—the Oscars, which completely robbed Aubrey of getting any of the other Big O's from Cordelia for over a month when her depressed lover didn't receive a nomination for *Chimera*.

Aubrey was extremely dissatisfied, and Cordelia was completely discontent.

By the second week of March, however, Cordelia's melancholy began to melt away like a snow-capped mountain does in spring.

Her shooting schedule returned to normal—*for her*—and she wanted Aubrey all the time. This presented Cordelia with a challenge. Aubrey was becoming known in the industry due to her performance in *Nightingales*, and someone—namely, the press—was bound to notice that an up-and-coming actress was spending an inordinate amount of time in Irvine.

Her solution was for Aubrey to rent the house next door, which 'suddenly' became vacant the last week in March. Perhaps it was the nightly and multiple releases of dopamine that she'd been denied for what felt like an eternity, but without reservation, and surely there should have been many after their Winter of Discontent, Aubrey's belongings took up residence next door, while her body took up permanent residence in Cordelia's bed.

Aubrey was deeply in love, and Cordelia was intensely in lust.

As summer approached and Cordelia's filming drew to a close, it was Aubrey who became despondent.

There was no discussion to be had—the day after *The Mountain Between Us* cast party, Aubrey would be left alone in Irvine to commute to Burbank for her new film while her lover joyfully flew off to London for over three months to do whatever it was that she did there that made her so happy to abandon Aubrey and their bed.

Yet, unlike Christmas, there were sporadic phone conversations that only increased her frustration and loneliness. Cordelia's voice always had a foreign, almost jubilant lilt when she called to 'check-in.' It certainly didn't sound like she was missed, nor was it ever mentioned. If Aubrey hadn't known better, she would've thought Cordelia had an English her there. And, whenever she dared to attempt to luridly describe exactly how much she and her body missed Cordelia, there was always someone within earshot.

Aubrey was deeply miserable, and Cordelia was completely ebullient.

The first week of September, it all started again, except now Aubrey knew what to expect.

There were the first few weeks of Cordelia's homesickness to endure, which was treated with her favorite foods and slow, intense lovemaking. Once the patient recovered, their life resumed its natural flow: weekdays were for work and occasional sex; weekends were for relaxation and, depending on her mood, as much sex as Cordelia wanted.

They never went out together publicly for obvious reasons —not that Cordelia willingly went anywhere other than to work. When Brenda forced her to attend a premiere or an award show, it was always done on Bradley's arm.

Aubrey, however, went out occasionally for drinks or dinner with her former roommates and current cast members. This allowed her to remain sane in an otherwise dysfunctional situation. Afterward, she would come home to always find Cordelia in bed, pretending to be asleep—pouting. Some nights, depending on how much 1800 she'd consumed, Aubrey would snuggle up against Cordelia's back and whisper the most profane things that sprung to mind. Other nights, depending on how little 1800 she drank, she would sleep on the very edge of the bed, signaling her displeasure at being in a relationship she was forbidden to acknowledge to anyone—including her own parents.

Although it was never discussed, Aubrey was sure that Cordelia's family had absolutely no idea they lived together. Without fail, every Sunday morning, promptly at seven, Cordelia's mother would call to apprise her oldest daughter of the happenings in the Wainwright household and, most importantly, the Wainwright Theater.

First, their dialogue revolved around her sisters' performances and then money. Not that she purposefully eavesdropped, but Aubrey never once heard Cordelia talk about her work or life in Los Angeles. The conversation ended the same each week: with a stern reminder to immediately call the youngest Wainwright, Ophy, who was away at boarding school in Cambridge. Cordelia's dutiful response to that command and whatever else she was instructed to do was, "Yes, Mother."

The only people permitted to visit the house were Geoffrey and Brenda, whom Cordelia begrudgingly told about their romance so that they could enable her to keep it a secret—not because she wanted them to share in their domestic bliss.

Bradley came and went as he wished and spent most of his time shooting on location in an often far, distant land. The only reason he ever came home was to keep up the appearance of a happy marriage and to take Cordelia to parties and award shows.

The only other person who knew what went on inside the house was their live-in housekeeper, Mrs. Holt, whom Cordelia had transplanted from her mother's home to her own when she married Bradley at age twenty-three.

Mrs. Holt was a middle-aged widow who spoke little, cooked the food Cordelia liked, and understood the true meaning of *'cleanliness is next to Godliness.'* Had she been twenty-five years younger, Aubrey would have been frightfully jealous of her, as she was Cordelia's ideal woman. Mrs. Holt's dedicated service and discretion were rewarded with free public school tuition for her four grandchildren and being dropped at their doorstep every Christmastime and at the start of the summer holiday.

Finally, there was to be no arguing or sentimentality—this was tantamount to Cordelia. When they disagreed, which was always about the same thing, the secrecy of their relationship, no harsh words were spoken. Instead, Cordelia pouted, and Aubrey, depending on the severity of her aggravation, either slept at the very edge of the bed or at the house next door.

Sentiment was not so easily avoided, though—at least for Aubrey.

When she'd mistakenly mentioned their first anniversary together, Cordelia had nonchalantly said, "Has it *only* been a year, then?" and said no more.

And, then, there was the word that should never be uttered—the *L-word*. This was especially difficult for Aubrey, as there were times when their lovemaking was so fulfilling that she wept or whispered some variation of 'I love you' into Cordelia's ear.

Cordelia's response was to act as though she didn't notice the tears or that she'd heard anything close to a declaration of love.

By the time their second Christmastime came around, Aubrey was fed up with pretending theirs was a relationship based solely on cohabitation and orgasms. In Aubrey's mind, it was one thing for Cordelia to behave as if she were nothing more than a colleague and a neighbor to the outside world and an entirely different matter to refuse to acknowledge her feelings in their own home. So, she expressly went against Cordelia's wishes and engaged in sentiment—and, most importantly, rebellion.

* * *

Dec. 18, 2009: Irvine, CA

The day before Cordelia was to leave for London, Aubrey, with the skeptical advice of Mrs. Holt, prepared a dinner consisting of roasted turkey, potatoes, cauliflower, parsnips, and a valiant effort at a traditional English Christmas cake.

As she examined the spiced cake from multiple viewpoints, Aubrey dubiously asked, "Um…is that how it's supposed to look?"

"Not exactly, Miss, but there's enough brandy in there that after a few bites, no one will care if it's a wee lopsided," the kind housekeeper assured her inexperienced apprentice. "What she *will* notice, no matter how snockered she gets, is the massive mess we've made in here, so we better get to cracking."

Thankfully, the *so, so, so white* kitchen was put back in order, and Aubrey had time to change her food-stained and flour-specked clothes by seven when Cordelia returned home from wrapping things up with Geoffrey at the studio before her departure.

As soon as Cordelia walked through the front door, she knew something was amiss.

First, she smelled the turkey—Mrs. Holt never cooked the night before they left for London. Second, she saw Aubrey wearing a way-too-short, spaghetti-strapped red dress, and a nervous smile—her usual at-home attire was shorts and an often wrinkled, oversized button-down shirt. And, then, there were the fidgeting hands—*one flex, double flex, shake out, and repeat.*

"'*Double, double toil and trouble, fire burn and cauldron bubble.'* You've been busy…no calls to the fire brigade, I hope," Cordelia joked as she walked behind Aubrey and slapped her ass just a little too hard to be judged as playful, which caused Aubrey to stiffen her back and, more importantly, her resolve.

"Mrs. Holt made sure of that," Aubrey said nervously as she followed Cordelia into the dining room, where two place settings of Wedgwood china had been laid atop a lace tablecloth.

Oh, bloody hell…

As Cordelia uneasily took her seat, a maelstrom of unpleasant scenarios ran through her racing mind, but the most disquieting ones were that Aubrey either wanted to get married or, perhaps worse, come to London with her.

"Isn't this the bit in the script where you offer me a drink after a long day at the office?"

"Do you want one?" Aubrey asked hopefully, and thought to herself: *If ever there was a time for you to abandon your teetotaling ways, this is it…and I could really use one…no, definitely more like three.*

It took all of Cordelia's polite, English breeding and restraint not to immediately demand that Aubrey ask for whatever she wanted so that she could say no and then go to bed.

For fuck's sake, she knows that I have an early flight in the morning.

Yet, she could see how anxious the girl standing before her was, with her always jittering hands, smoothing down the tablecloth as though it were about to drift away.

"Do I need one? Stop hovering and sit down so we can eat."

There was no dinner conversation other than a back-handed compliment: "This is surprisingly not so bad."

Instead of words passing between them, there were stolen glances and a few tight, awkward smiles. Not even Aubrey's sad, misshapen spiced cake warranted a witty remark from Cordelia, although she did make two very loud gulps when she struggled to swallow a few bites of it and wash them down with milk.

Quite indelicately put, it was like a Mexican standoff—whoever blinked first might blow up their life together: *Was it worth it?*

With all the food choked down and the table furiously cleared by Aubrey—Cordelia was thankful her expensive tableware had made it to the kitchen intact—it was time to get down to brass tacks.

"What's the next scene? Am I to play it as though I am in a Bergman or Cassavetes film?"

Don't let her bait you, Aubrey thought as she placed a small, gold-wrapped rectangular box on the table before Cordelia. "Merry Christmas."

Thank God—it's not a ring box!

Cordelia opened the box and found a vintage black Conway Stewart fountain pen trimmed in 14k gold that closely resembled the one that she used of her father's.

"Thank you, Sweetheart, it's lovely. But, I didn't—"

"Read the inscription, Cordy," Aubrey cut her off before she could tell her what she already knew—that, yet, *again*, there was no gift for her.

"Para mi amor, the Scrivener."

If it were possible to be both paralyzed by fear and at the same time moved by, dare she say it, *sentiment*, this was the state Cordelia now found herself in. She knew Aubrey loved her—she'd whispered it in her ear many nights—but this was said in such a way that Cordelia couldn't ignore it.

Thankfully, the china is tucked safely away in the kitchen.

"Is this why you've taken up cooking…to starve me to death like Bartleby?"

Painfully realizing that the words she longed to hear were not forthcoming, Aubrey had to quickly decide if she wanted to flee from or fight for what she wanted. She chose to fight and bolted upright out of her chair.

Aubrey pointed a determined, non-fidgety index finger at Cordelia. "I'm going to speak, and you're going to listen, got it? Nod your head if you understand."

This clear, matter-of-fact command was enough to compel Cordelia to dutifully assent.

"I love you, Cordy, and I don't care if you can't/won't say it back to me for whatever fucked up reason you've cooked up in that dysfunctional mind of yours. You don't have to tell me it because I *know* it. I know it when you smile at me. I know it when you kiss me. I know it when you make love to me. I know it because you keep me here even though your greatest fear is that people we don't even fucking know will find out that you love me!"

There were no tears or histrionics—just Aubrey's unyielding resolve.

"So, this is how things are going to go from now on: One, whenever we are in this house, I will not hide my feelings—good or bad, people fucking argue, Cordy! Two, I will tell my parents about us—that is non-negotiable. Three, we will buy furniture for this house that has actual color in it—and not fucking black! Four, this will be the *last* Christmas and New Year's Eve we spend apart—and you *will* buy me fucking gifts, even for my birthday and our anniversary! Five, I don't care what elaborate cover story you and Geoffrey have to concoct; you will *not* leave me here for over three fucking months every summer to visit your family."

There Aubrey stood in all her glory: straight-backed, still hands, and so not joking.

Where did this confident, ultimatum-delivering woman come from? Sure, she could be bossy and demanding in bed, but what happened to the awkward, fidgety girl with whom I just ate that poor excuse for an English Christmas dinner? This all seems so…familiar.

"Do you understand?" Aubrey asked, interrupting Cordelia's thoughts.

"Yes, but—"

"No fucking buts, Cordy!"

Cordelia quickly nodded to show that she understood; she was too afraid not to.

"Now, tell me how nice I look!" Aubrey demanded, slowly twirling around in a circle.

"You look very nice, Sweetheart."

God, I love her legs…and that ass.

"Now, you're going to get up, and we're going to go to bed and you're going to make love to me like you're not going to see me for weeks. And then you're going to look me in the eyes when I say that I love you, and then you will nod. Got it?"

"Yes, Sweetheart, I would *prefer* that."

CHAPTER FOUR

"A Summer's Tale"

Jan. 10, 2010-May 7, 2010: Irvine, CA

It had been nearly six months since Aubrey had issued her demands to Cordelia. And, for the most part, she'd acquiesced. While she still refused, for whatever *insane* reason known only to herself, to audibly admit that she loved Aubrey, she showed it with her actions—and her nods.

When Aubrey's parents called from Vermont, she said hello and asked about their garden—although the idea of people digging around in the dirt for 'fun' was anathema to her.

For her twenty-fifth birthday in January, Aubrey got an embossed Letts' planner with a handwritten note, etched in black ink: *'Now you have no excuse to be late ever again, Sweetheart.'*

And, while it had not been specifically listed in the litany of commands, out of a sense of precaution and self-preservation, Cordelia even gave Aubrey a Valentine's gift of Burberry perfume, with yet another handwritten note, etched in black ink: *'Now you have no excuse to ever smell like a French whore again, Sweetheart.'*

These notes often led to arguments, which Cordelia had fully intended. Although, she felt Aubrey got a bit too heated over the French whore one when she'd thrown the perfume box back at her.

Cordelia much *preferred* controlled chaos to Aubrey's unpredictable fits of fury at small things like her: working too late at the studio, not wanting to watch Katherine Heigl movies, or refusing to try new foods. Aubrey did many things that drove Cordelia completely mad: wet towels and clothes thrown on the floor, her resistance to coasters, brushing crumbs off countertops and onto the floor, and constantly complaining that they never went anywhere together. Yet, she rarely said anything about those irritating habits, choosing instead to pick up, wipe off, sweep up, and go down on her lover.

When *they'd* redecorated the living and dining rooms in *cheerful* colors, Cordelia didn't complain as she watched Bradley and his friends move her beautifully pristine white furniture to Aubrey's uninhabited home next door.

Yet, when Aubrey suggested they redo the kitchen, Cordelia put her foot down.

"I know you do not cook, Sweetheart, but food is a breeding ground for bacteria, and white is the best color to detect its perniciousness."

For Cordelia's peace of mind, Aubrey allowed the kitchen to remain *so, so, so white*.

The only edict other than Christmastime that had not yet been dealt with was Cordelia's yearly three-month summer holiday in London. As there was absolutely no question about whether she would go, she had to work out some scenario where it seemed perfectly normal for Aubrey to go along, too.

This took an inordinate amount of scheming on the part of *Frick and Frack*. Still, they finally concocted a plausible cover story: Aubrey's next role would be as a young actress in a Shakespearean theater troupe—they even got one of Geoffrey's friends to write a screenplay. And who better to live with and shadow than one of the best-known Shakespearean actresses alive, Beatrice Wainwright, who just happened to be the mother of her good friend, Cordelia.

After much debate, Cordelia went to London the second week in May, when her film wrapped up ahead of schedule. Aubrey knew, of course, that this was precisely why Cordelia had worked even more hours than usual that spring. She chalked it up to Cordelia's anxiety about her meeting the Wainwrights. Aubrey was sure that Cordelia still hadn't told her mother that a naked woman was trying to sleep beside her as they had their weekly Sunday morning chats.

She probably needs time to mentally prepare, Aubrey told herself.

Since her film wouldn't be finished until the end of May, it only made sense that Aubrey would join Cordelia in London after that.

* * *

May 28, 2010: St. Albans, England

There was no greeting at Heathrow, just a car service instructed to bring Aubrey to St. Albans.

The Wainwrights did not live in London proper but resided approximately twenty minutes outside the city on a Georgian estate in the Hertfordshire countryside. It was secluded, private, and quiet—Cordelia's version of heaven on Earth.

Aubrey couldn't believe her eyes when the town car pulled into the circular drive. Yes, she was surprised by how massive the house was, but she was even more intrigued by the woman standing right outside it dressed in white Barbour linen trousers and a green silk blouse—colors she'd never seen Cordelia wear outside a movie set.

"Hello, Sweetheart." Cordelia gave Aubrey a quick kiss on the cheek, instructed the driver where to drop his passenger's luggage, and then took the crook of Aubrey's arm to guide her toward the front door.

Aubrey leaned over and raspily whispered into Cordelia's ear, "You look *very* nice in those pants, *mi amor*."

Her response was an apprehensive smile. "Please behave yourself, Sweetheart."

Did she just politely tell me to shut the fuck up? Aubrey's eyes narrowed, her head cocked to the side, and she said no more.

As soon as they entered the house, Cordelia's family met them.

"Right, well, so, these are my sisters, Miranda and Portia." Cordelia halfheartedly waved at two carbon copies of herself: tall, thin, strawberry-blond, striking blue eyes, and wearing tailored clothing. "And this is my mother, Beatrice."

While Aubrey had seen her in photographs and numerous PBS and BBC broadcasts, she was struck by how much presence Beatrice commanded in person. Beatrice also had no qualms about letting Aubrey see that she was examining her from head to foot.

As Aubrey made this observation, she heard Cordelia say, "Wainwrights, this is my friend, Aubrey."

Her head snapped back like a rubber band towards Cordelia, and her fiery light-brown eyes said what she could not say aloud: *You fucking, coward.*

Always on cue, Beatrice saw the look of death her eldest daughter had been dealt and stepped in.

"Cut! No, no, that simply won't do, Delia. Start again."

Aubrey stifled a laugh and thought, *Oh, we're definitely going to be friends.*

"Mother, what are you doing? Are you having a stroke?" Cordelia asked.

"What? Isn't that what they do when you flub a line in your vulgar business?"

"I do not…'flub' lines…" Cordelia stammered.

"Of course you do, Darling—that's why you ran off to the world of endless retakes in the first place. We've all seen you work without a net. Still, no one can pull a stray line from the ether like you—she does that, Aubrey, does she not?" Beatrice knowingly asked.

"Occasionally." Aubrey was amazed—she'd never heard anyone speak to Cordelia like this.

"One of her *many* affectations. Really, Darling, what did contractions ever do to you to make you hate them so?" Beatrice sarcastically asked, which made Aubrey and the sisters laugh.

Cordelia was rendered speechless by her mother's apparent need to dress her down in front of everyone.

"Nevertheless, your sisters and I know you don't have any 'friends,' Delia. Although there was that one girl at school who'd sit with you at lunch..." When she couldn't recall the name, Beatrice snapped her fingers twice and pointed at Miranda to assist her.

"Sloane."

"Sloane! Such a sad child, really...no wonder you got on so well...but her mother did have hopes of being more than a bit player at the theater, so there's that."

After completely eviscerating Cordelia in a matter of minutes, she turned her attention back to Aubrey. "So, Aubrey, since we *know* that you're *not* Delia's 'friend,' we were wondering exactly what you are: minion, prop, or enabler?"

"Um...all three," Aubrey sardonically retorted.

"Oh, my, then you must be exceptional indeed!" Beatrice exclaimed in her best stage voice and knowingly glared at Cordelia. "You must be exhausted after such a long flight. I'll show you to your room."

"I can do that, Mother; she is my guest, after all." Cordelia's voice sounded defeated when she said it.

"Nonsense! Your retakes may pay the bills, but this is still my house. Besides, you need to get to the station to pick up Ophy. Come along, Aubrey." She held out her hand to the young woman she had just rescued and brushed past Cordelia, wearing a victorious smile.

* * *

"So, here we are. Dresser, chest, *closet*, bed...the mattress is practically an antique, but...if you come through here," Beatrice walked into a shared bathroom and slid open the adjoining door, "you will find one that is way too rigid but disinfected weekly."

When Aubrey walked through the bathroom and into the bedroom next to hers, she saw an almost exact replica of the one she shared with Cordelia in Irvine.

"So, you know…"

"That my daughter is incredibly stupid? Of course, the doctors confirmed it at a very young age."

"And, you don't…mind?" Aubrey asked.

"We're a theater family, Dear; many fruits have fallen from our proverbial tree." Beatrice sat on Cordelia's bed and motioned for Aubrey to do the same. "I've had my suspicions about Delia for ages. No one *prefers* being asexual, not even someone as preoccupied with germs and bacteria as my daughter. When Geoffrey told me how she was treating you, I knew instantly that she fancied you—she just needed a shove, you see, so—"

"It was you!" Aubrey exclaimed as though she'd unmasked the culprit on a crime series. "Cordy never willingly invites anyone to the house."

A wide, Cheshire cat grin spread across Beatrice's face. "*Cordy*, is it? Surely, you've lived with *Cordy* long enough to know that often she needs to be told what to do. I suspect that's exactly how you ended up in her bed and then here."

Aubrey's response was a guilty, crooked smile.

Beatrice pointed at a black, gold-inlaid desk in front of the bed. "Do you see that hideous desk with all the small drawers over there?"

"Yes, she has one just like it at home." Aubrey suddenly blushed, recalling that it was up against that desk at home that she'd given Cordelia the release she *desperately* needed their first night together.

"Of course she does." Beatrice shook her head in exasperation. "Do you know why?"

"Because she's borderline OCD."

At this quip, Beatrice boisterously laughed. "You must love her—there's nothing borderline about any of her *peculiarities*. It belonged to her father—she worshiped him. That desk is Delia in an uncracked nutshell."

Beatrice got up from the bed and stood next to the desk in question. "It's how she slogs her way through life—compartmentalizing. Each drawer represents something or someone.

"On this side, we have Los Angeles," she pointed to the left side of the desk and then at each of its four small drawers. "Minions: Keisha, poor girl; Props: Bradley, the *husband*; Enablers: Brenda, horrid woman; and Career: Geoffrey, although he *definitely* fits into the enabler drawer, too."

Then she pointed to the right side of the desk and its corresponding drawers. "This is London. Competitors: Portia and Miranda; Hindrances: Me; Inhibitors: Ophy; and Redundancy: the Wainwright." After a dramatic pause, she looked at Aubrey and asked, "So, Dear, in which compartment do you think she's filed you?"

Aubrey got up from the bed and stood before the desk, staring intently at all of the drawers. "That one." Aubrey pointed at a large drawer directly in the middle of the desk, surrounded by the smaller ones.

Beatrice tapped the drawer. "Go on, then, open it."

When Aubrey tried to slide it open, it was locked.

With a sigh, Beatrice looked at Aubrey. "Trust me, Dear, you don't want to be filed in that one—that's where her regrets are kept." Then, she placed her hand on the smooth writing surface of the desk. "No, what you want—what we *all* want—is for you to be here. That's where the curtain *finally* falls on this never-ending production of *Tartuffe*."

Aubrey had no idea what that meant, but she knew that she didn't like the way Beatrice said it or the look of resignation on her face when she said it.

Beatrice changed the subject, realizing she'd brought a dark cloud to an otherwise sunny day. "I'll leave you to it, then. Delia should be back with Ophy around half past five. Rest up—she'll have overdosed on sweets on the train."

* * *

After unpacking and settling in her room, Aubrey decided to get acquainted with the house where she'd spend the next three months.

It was a grand house, decorated tastefully, with warm colors, lots of expensive wood and crown molding, antiques, and Persian rugs. It was so unlike Cordelia's home in Irvine, before and even after they redecorated. There was still the matter of the identical bedrooms, minus Oscar and that disturbing Ophelia painting.

That's even weird for Cordy.

As she was walking down a hallway back toward where she'd first met the Wainwrights, a perky child wearing a navy blue jumper with St. Mary's School embroidered on it came bouncing down the hall.

"Hiya, my name's Ophelia Wainwright, but everyone calls me Ophy. I'm ten."

She looked like all the other Wainwrights, just shorter and more effervescent. Her strawberry-blond hair was in French braids.

Aubrey held out her hand. "It's very nice to meet you, Ophy. I'm Aubrey Taylor, and I'm twenty-five."

"Do you like Enola Holmes?" Ophy enthusiastically inquired, declining to shake hands.

Aubrey had no idea. "Is she a character in Harry Potter?"

This response elicited a scoff—*from a child!*

"She's a detective, not a wizard! She solves crimes like her brother Sherlock."

Before Aubrey could overcome her poor first impression, Cordelia strolled down the hallway.

"There you are, Ophy… Oh, I see you two have met." She nervously smiled when she saw Aubrey.

"Dilly, she doesn't know who Enola Holmes is!" Ophy declared, clearly outraged at Aubrey's ignorance of children's literature.

Cordelia suppressed a laugh when she saw Aubrey's unwarranted embarrassment. "Well, not everyone is as well-read as you, Ophy. You will have to lend her one of your books."

"I'll be right back!"

She exuberantly ran off, presumably to fetch a book for their unlearned houseguest.

When she was gone, Cordelia walked closer to Aubrey, but not nearly close enough for Aubrey's liking.

"One too many Fruittellas on the train. Did you get settled?"

"You mean in *my* room?" If her tone didn't say how displeased she was, then her narrowed eyes and set jaw did.

Why must she always be so difficult?

"Aubrey…it's—"

Aubrey cut her off, "Adjoined to yours? Yes, your *mother* showed me."

"Did she now?" Cordelia felt uneasy when she imagined how that conversation must have gone.

"Why do I need my own room if everyone knows where I'll *really* be sleeping and—"

Cordelia cut her off this time. "*Everyone* doesn't know."

Almost on cue, Ophy came running back down the hallway, book in hand.

"Here," she shoved a copy of *The Case of the Missing Marquess* into Aubrey's hands. "This is the first one. There are six total, and the last one is called *The Case of the Gypsy Goodbye*. It just came out, but I haven't read it yet. Dilly and I always read them together."

To make a point to Aubrey, Cordelia looked down at the in-house Wainwright librarian. "So, Ophy, what juicy dirt have you brought back from St. Mary's?" Then, she leaned against the wall, crossed her arms, and looked directly, and pointedly, at her lover.

All at once, words rapidly fell out of Ophy's over-sugar-ingested mouth. "Penelope's parents are getting divorced. Mrs. Bright went daft for her yoga instructor. Oh, and Celeste isn't coming back for fall term because her daddy took money from his bank, and now they're poor."

"My, my, you could have your own column at the *Daily Mail*," Cordelia said to Ophy, but mainly to a very silent Aubrey.

"Silly Dilly! You know I'm going to write mysteries!" Ophy declared indignantly.

Finally, Aubrey had something to say. "I thought all Wainwright girls grew up to be actresses?" She knew this was a sore subject for Cordelia.

"Dilly says acting is for talentless neurotics. You're an actress, right?"

The snarky way she said this made Aubrey think instantly that strawberry-blond hair and blue eyes weren't the only traits the Wainwright girls shared.

Cordelia bit her lip when she saw the stunned, insulted look on Aubrey's face, and then she patted her mini-me on the head. "Good girl."

* * *

After a dinner of the same English food that she ate nearly every night in Irvine, Aubrey was ready for bed—and Cordelia.

The dinner conversation revolved around Ophy's spring term and the Wainwright's fall lineup. Aubrey met Miranda's husband, Clark, who was the theater manager. He was a quiet forty-year-old man wholly intimidated by his mother-in-law: "Yes, Beatrice, you're quite right.'"

Cordelia mostly conversed with Ophy and said little to anyone else. This irritated Aubrey to no end because they were seated beside one another and because Cordelia quickly jerked her hand away whenever Aubrey brushed her left hand against her lover's right one.

"If you don't mind, I think I'm ready for bed. It's been a long day." Aubrey feigned a yawn.

Beatrice took the hint: *She is an actress.* "Of course, Dear."

Cordelia was oblivious. "Goodnight. I will probably be at the theater with Clark when you get up, but Mother can keep you entertained."

Aubrey's head sharply tilted toward Cordelia and she thought, *What the fuck?*

Not wanting their first impression of her to be that of a horny, *neurotic* Hollywood actress, Aubrey stood and bid them all goodnight. And, then, she waited—and waited, and waited in the bedroom. As Aubrey lay, well, waiting in Cordelia's bed for hours, she kept staring angrily at that pigeonhole desk, which was staring right back at her. She felt as if it were mocking her.

After four sleepless hours, she got out of bed, put on her red silk robe, and looked for Cordelia. She found Beatrice sitting in a winged-back burgundy chair, reading a book in the family's living room.

When Beatrice saw her, she put down the book. "You're up late, Dear. I thought you'd be knackered, but I suppose it's a big time difference between here and Los Angeles. Perhaps a nightcap will help—just promise me you'll brush your teeth before you go to bed. You know how *she* is."

"About *that*..."

A look of something close to pity crossed Beatrice's face when she realized it wasn't a drink Aubrey wanted or needed. "Oh, I see...follow me, Dear."

A few minutes later, they stood outside Ophy's open bedroom door and saw Cordelia fast asleep in the youngest Wainwright's bed. A copy of *The Case of the Gypsy Goodbye* was hanging precariously from Ophy's sleeping hand.

Beatrice looked pityingly at Aubrey. "Our replacements get younger every year, do they not?"

* * *

May 29-June 2, 2010: St. Albans, England

For four very long days, Aubrey spent most of her time with Beatrice, learning about the history of the house, the family, and the Wainwright. Cordelia spent her days at the theater with Clark, going over finances, the upkeep of the theater, and dealing with advertisements for the fall schedule. Cordelia subsidized the theater with her own money and spent her holidays ensuring it was well spent.

There was no summer program at the theater, so in the evenings, when they returned home, always at half past six, the family ate dinner together and then spent the rest of the night playing games in the living room—namely charades and/or Bridge.

Much to Aubrey's consternation, Ophy was always Cordelia's partner: *What ten-year-old plays Bridge?*

Aubrey waited for Cordelia to come to bed for four incredibly lonely nights, but she never did. Each night at nine o'clock, Beatrice would announce that it was Ophy's bedtime, and then Ophy and Cordelia would go off together to Ophy's room to read about Enola Holmes. They did this every night. And, every night, Cordelia would fall asleep in Ophy's bed.

On the rare occasion that Aubrey caught Cordelia in the morning before she left for town, promptly at eight every morning, she would make Cordelia promise to come to their bed that night. Cordelia dutifully nodded.

Beatrice watched all this silently, waiting for Aubrey to put her foot down. When this didn't happen, she took matters into her own hands.

"It's past your bedtime, Ophy. Go brush your teeth and wash your face, and I'll be in to tuck you in."

Beatrice never tucked Ophy in since Cordelia was already there.

"But Dilly and I are going to finish *The Case of the Gypsy Goodbye* tonight, Mama!" Ophy protested.

"Dilly's going to sleep in her own bed tonight...aren't you, Dilly?" Beatrice pointedly looked at her eldest daughter and then slyly slid her eyes toward Aubrey's chair.

"Right, well, Mother, I did promise her..." Cordelia stammered.

"How long is that bloody book? It's not Jane Austen, for heaven's sake! And, besides, weren't you complaining about having a crick in your neck earlier? Falling asleep in Ophy's tiny bed can't be good for that, and you *always* drift off when she reads to you. I am certain you will find sleeping in your bed much more *pleasurable*."

Ophy countered quite rationally, "We'll just read in Dilly's bed then. It's big enough for the both of us."

All eyes in the room immediately focused on Cordelia—most especially Aubrey's fiery light-brown ones.

"Right, well, I don't think Flora's changed the linens since I haven't been sleeping in it—there could be dust mites! We better do our reading in your bed. Now, go do what Mama said, and I'll be in soon."

"Promise?"

Cordelia smiled and crossed her heart. "Whenever have I not been precise in my promise keeping to you, Darling?"

Once assured that her reading partner would soon join her, Ophy said goodnight to everyone and skipped off to bed.

When the child was out of sight, Aubrey stood up from her chair and slowly walked over to Cordelia, sitting on the couch Ophy had just vacated. She crossed her arms, and in a steely voice, said, "You're slipping, *Ms. Wainwright*. Isn't that the same line you used on me this morning when you swore you'd sleep in *our* bed tonight?"

"Aubrey!" Cordelia jolted off the couch, outraged that she wanted to discuss their sleeping arrangements in front of the entire family.

"Shut the fuck up! I put up with your closeted bullshit in LA, but I'm not gonna do it in this house where *everyone* over the age of ten knows that we do more than sleep in the same bed. I've been here almost a week, and you haven't given me more than a peck on the cheek. Not to mention that we haven't made love in weeks! I need you…*desperately, mi amor.*"

And very much like their very first kiss, she grabbed Cordelia's face in her hands and brought her pouty lips down on Cordelia's like a vice grip.

And, just as before, Cordelia shoved her away, stunned by her boldness.

"Are you drunk? Stop it! We'll talk about…*this*…in the morning," she said in a raised voice as she started to leave the room without acknowledging what everyone had just witnessed.

But before her lover could make an embarrassed retreat, Aubrey grabbed Cordelia's wrist, spun her back around, and tightened her grip on the struggling wrist.

Cordelia was speechless.

"Um, no, we won't. I'm going to speak, and you're going to listen, got it? Nod your head if you understand."

Apprehensively, Cordelia nodded, but thought: *Not this again.*

"I *love* you more than anything in the world, Cordy, but if you don't come to *our* bed right *now*, I'm leaving you in the morning and going back to LA, where I'll break the lease for that vacant house next to *ours*, and then buy myself a condo in the city—in a lesbian-only community, and I'll have sex with everyone in it and never change the sheets once. Do you understand me?"

Cordelia warily nodded.

Portia, Miranda, and Clark couldn't believe their collective bulging eyes. There was only one other person who spoke to Cordelia like this.

Beatrice smiled and stated the obvious, "That's quite a vivid image, Darling."

* * *

The following day was a Saturday, so Cordelia didn't have to get up early and go into town. This was fortunate because very little sleeping had been done the previous night.

Each time she thought she might have finally fully satisfied Aubrey's out-of-control libido, she soon learned that it was apparently limitless. Every time she was just mere moments from falling off into a stupor, she would feel one of Aubrey's legs seductively sliding up her own, which was soon followed by caressing fingertips down the length of her spine, and a raspy voice in her ear, '*mi amor.*' If there ever was a time Cordelia wished that she were a man, this was it.

When she was finally permitted to drift off to sleep in exhaustion, she did so in a Stage 4 coma-esque state. Like her spent lover, Aubrey was also metaphorically dead to the world. But unlike Cordelia, hers was a result of a dopamine overdose. This is why they didn't hear the knock on their locked bedroom door.

Since she slept on the side of the bed facing the bathroom, Aubrey's face was the first one that Ophy saw when she entered *that* unlocked door. Perhaps it was out of shock, but more likely jealousy that anyone other than herself would dare to sleep in Dilly's bed, which caused her to walk over and impolitely poke Aubrey's bare shoulder.

Lazily, Aubrey opened one eye to find two extremely wide, accusatory blue eyes staring daggers down at her.

Fuck!

As she was completely naked under the down comforter, she had no other option but to attempt to rouse her lover with quick, haphazard slaps on her bare ass. "Cordy…babe, wake up…"

Cordelia was having none of it. "No, I am tired. Did you not get enough last night?"

Aubrey embarrassedly smiled at her angry rival and said more forcefully, "I'm serious, Cordelia! Wake up…*now!*"

Again, Cordelia refused to roll over. "For fuck's sake, use your hand or that vibrator I *know* you keep in the drawer!"

"What's a vibrator?" a familiar, oh-so-not raspy voice asked.

Instantaneously, Cordelia became fully conscious. Without turning over, lest she expose herself to unwanted questions, she snapped her fingers twice and pointed to her side of the bed.

Once Ophy stood before her with her arms crossed tightly against her chest, Cordelia asked, "How did you get in here, Ophy?"

"Through the loo…"

They had not thought to lock *that* door.

With a perturbed tone and jerk of her head in Aubrey's direction, she demanded, "Why is *she* sleeping in your bed?"

"Her bed is old and uncomfortable," Cordelia reasoned.

"But why is she *naked*?"

"Yes, well…do you remember that program we watched about cross-contamination? It's like that. She didn't want to transfer the germs from her bed to mine."

"But, why are you naked, *too*?"

"My goodness, you're quite the detective this morning," Cordelia flattered her, frantically trying to stall for enough time to come up with a plausible answer.

"I bet you wish she were talentless and neurotic now," Aubrey joked from the other side of the bed.

Ophy was not amused. "Yes, a good detective notices everything—like you have two scratches on your back."

As if this statement of fact were not embarrassing enough, Ophy leaned over Cordelia's frame and jabbed her index finger into the evidence.

Goddammit, Aubrey!

"Is there? Well, I must've dreamt about those dirty dust mites and scratched myself," Cordelia said trying not to blush.

It was abundantly evident by the look on Ophy's skeptical face that she wasn't buying what Cordelia was selling. Professor Moriarty was clearly cornered by a ten-year-old girl.

"All right, Inspector Holmes, I see that you'll not be satisfied until you have my full confession. If you go into the loo and wait 'til I call you, I'll answer all of your questions. Shoo…and slide the door closed, if you please."

Once the Grand Inquisitor was safely stowed in the bathroom, Cordelia forcefully and deliberately whipped the covers back onto Aubrey and angrily whispered, "This is all your and Mother's fucking fault!"

Aubrey flipped over onto her back, propped herself up with her elbows, and watched as Cordelia scrambled to get dressed.

"Calm down, Cordy. It's not—"

Cordelia cut her off, "*Yes,* it is!"

Then she snatched Aubrey's wrinkled button-down shirt and panties off the bedroom floor and threw them so quickly at Aubrey that they hit her right smack in the face.

"For fuck's sake, clothe yourself!"

"That lesbian-only complex is sounding better every fucking minute." Aubrey did as she was told and hastily buttoned up the shirt.

Somewhat decently attired, Cordelia called Ophy back into the crime scene and pointed at the bed. Ophy looked menacingly at Aubrey, sitting up in bed now, and sat on the opposite side.

To calm her raging nerves, Cordelia took a deep breath and nervously ran her hands through her messy hair. "Before we start the interrogation, I will ask you a few questions. First: You know who I am outside this house, right—to people like Celeste and Penelope and all the other girls at school and their parents?"

"Yes, you're Cordelia Wainwright—you live in Hollywood and make films," Ophy stated matter-of-factly.

"Right, but who am I when I am not in Hollywood—when I am here at the house?"

"You're Dilly, silly."

"Right, here I get to be the real me, not some talentless, neurotic actress who only exists to entertain people. Here, I do not have to pretend to be your Dilly, a daughter, a sister, or someone's partner. I cherish being those things to the people I love more than anything but I am selfish and do not want to share my happiness with anyone outside this house. Do you understand?"

Cordelia hoped to God that she did.

"Yes, it's just for us," Ophy answered.

"Good, girl," Cordelia said, patting Ophy on the head.

Then, she sat beside Aubrey on the bed and took her hand into her own. "You found Aubrey in my bed…nude…because she is my partner, and whenever we are in the same house, we sleep together…often, naked. That means that I cannot sleep in your bed every night—and, *no*, you cannot sleep with us, either—and that before you come into our room, you must first knock—just like you do with Miranda and Clark. Got it?"

"Yes, I must knock first so I don't see you naked or having sex like Miranda and Clark."

Aubrey squeezed Cordelia's hand to discourage her lover from asking what she knew was running wildly through her uptight mind: *How do you know what sex is?*

"Hmm… So, have I answered all your questions, Inspector?"

Ophy took a moment to consider her checklist. "Almost. You never said what a vibrator is."

Aubrey suppressed a laugh and squeezed Cordelia's hand once more.

"It's a massager," Cordelia answered, again trying not to blush.

"For the pain in your neck?"

This time, she squeezed Aubrey's hand. "*Precisely*. Now, off you go," Cordelia said, standing up and walking Ophy over to the door.

Once she was gone, Cordelia wearily leaned back against the door. "Thank God, that is over."

Aubrey was beaming at her. "And to think I was jealous of the only person that could force you to admit that you 'love' and 'cherish' your 'partner,'" she said as she got out of bed.

Cordelia rolled her eyes. "Stop looking at me like some love-struck schoolgirl. You and your co-conspirator got what you wanted."

"God, I love your mother!" Aubrey exclaimed and then propped herself up on the desk. "And I adore you on this side of the desk."

"I think you mean pond, Sweetheart. Don't sit on that," Cordelia instructed as she sat on the bed.

"Why—is it *improper*?" Aubrey said as she started unbuttoning the front of her shirt.

Cordelia *knew* that tone. "Stop messing about."

With her shirt now fully open, she then slid her right hand inside of her panties. "Hmm…but I'm waiting for you right…here."

Not amused, Cordelia reminded her, "You know that was my father's desk, right? Get off there!"

"That's what I'm doing," Aubrey wickedly rasped.

"That's not what I meant."

Aubrey giggled and removed her hand from inside her panties. "Yes, it's one of the many reasons I love you. I'll come down for you on two conditions: we lock the door, and you say *IT*…to me," she bargained.

"Does it really count if *IT* is compelled with manipulation?"

"Oh, Ms. Wainwright, I love it when you talk dirty to me," she said as she started to move her hand back down toward her panties.

For fuck's sake, she is going to defile Father's desk!

Cordelia quickly stood and offered her hand to her blackmailer. "All right, I love you. Now come down."

At that, Aubrey shook her head and seductively laughed as Cordelia helped her off the desk and locked the door.

When Cordelia turned around, Aubrey waited for her on the bed. "You first, *mi amor.*"

Cordelia nodded her head as she walked toward the bed. Then she gave Aubrey a smile that melted her heart.

"I would definitely *prefer* that, *My Love.* I'm exhausted."

Part II

Beatrice

CHAPTER FIVE

"Macbeatrice"

Feb. 21, 2017: Los Angeles, CA

"To be fair, Cordelia, I'm only saying what Aubrey herself has said numerous times. When I interviewed her last week, she said that you taught her everything she knows about being an actress. As a matter of fact, she said that you're probably the greatest actress she has ever met," Patti said.

I bet she did.

"I hope my mother does not see that interview." Cordelia scornfully laughed.

"Speaking of your mother, the grand dame of Shakespeare, Beatrice Wainwright, it was under her that you studied acting at your family's theater in London. What was that like?" Patti asked.

Unadulterated hell, you fucking cow.

"My mother's tutelage was quite instructive, Patti. Without her firm hand guiding me through the rigors and intricacies of stage acting, I can say with *absolute* and *complete* confidence that I would not be the actress I am today. My successes as an actress are owed entirely to her."

* * *

June 1997-Nov. 1998: London & St. Albans, England

"Why must you *always* be so stiff, Darling?" Beatrice observed as she walked in a circular motion around Cordelia, who was standing centre-stage at the Wainwright Theater. "I blame your father for insisting on sending you to an all-girls school—had you gone to school with blokes, you probably would've been shagged by now and have some notion of the meaning of a relaxed state."
Silence.
Unlike most of her schoolmates, Cordelia wasn't spending her summer holiday traipsing about the continent, drinking, smoking, and shagging anything that she could get her hands on. No, she had the unique pleasure of spending hers in a hot, dusty, *dirty* theater with the woman she dreamt about murdering every night in her sleep. She'd had precisely one weekend off after completing her secondary education at St. Mary's before her A-Levels instruction from hell began with Lady Macbeth.
"Do you masturbate, Darling?"
"Mother!" Cordelia shrieked, blushing.
"No, of course you don't. Perhaps we should take you to one of those shops for your birthday. A vibrator might help with *this*," Beatrice said, waving her hand derisively at Cordelia's torso. "Don't worry; we can pick up extra hand sanitizer, too."
Silence.
This is how Cordelia spent the first three weeks of her apprenticeship. An apprenticeship that she had no desire whatsoever to serve. Had she been allowed to choose for herself, she would have chosen to spend her summer listening to audiobooks on finance and not John Barton's *Playing Shakespeare*. Natural speech; language and character; the subtlety of sarcasm, irony, and ambiguity; and, Cordelia's particular favorite, connecting

one's performance with the audience. It was maddening. *I despise iambic pentameter!* By no stretch of anyone's demented imagination did Cordelia wish to become Judi Dench—or worse, her mother. She wanted to be Jayne-Anne Gadhia, the co-founder of Virgin Money.

"You look a bit peaked, Darling. Did you eat this morning?" Beatrice asked, noticing that her daughter's pallor was unusually ashen—*even for her.*

"It's bloody stifling in here, Mother," Cordelia said weakly.

"Yes, but one would think your color wouldn't be so gr—"

Before she could finish saying 'gray,' Cordelia's legs buckled, and her body crumpled to the floor like an accordion.

"Goddamnit, Delia! How often must you be told not to lock your bloody knees!"

* * *

Henry couldn't help but notice that the mood at the dining table was even more somber than usual. Each successive day of *training* darkened the mood of not only his daughter but also the house. Mother and daughter were especially reticent this evening, and several times, he saw what could only be described as death glares pass between the two.

"Everything go well today, Delia?" he asked nonchalantly, as he subconsciously rubbed his left cheek—Cordelia had an abrasion on her own from hitting it on her way down to the *so, so, so solid* wood stage of the Wainwright.

Silence.

"Apparently, the nuns at St. Mary's have instructed her well on how to keep her knees locked," Beatrice sharply answered the question her husband so obviously wanted to ask. "Rest assured, Dear, she thoroughly disinfected it with an entire tube of Neosporin when we came home."

"Right, well, perhaps we might let her work with me in the office tomorrow. Give her a break of sorts from her…*training.* We are putting together some mock-ups for the fall advertisements."

"Could I, Papa?" Cordelia eagerly asked, finally breaking her silence.

"Nonsense! What does she need to know about advertisements other than how to stand and have her photo taken for them?" Beatrice determinedly said to her husband. She then turned her attention back to Cordelia, sitting directly across the table, gripping her knife and fork so tightly in her hands that Beatrice knew she was on the cusp of exploding. "So, in a way, Darling, we are preparing you for that now. Standing upright without fainting is an important aspect of being both an actress and creating good advertisements."

Wedgwood china is usually quite durable because it is made of bone ash, which reinforces the structure of a dish, yet when three pounds of Arthur Price cutlery is slammed down onto it with the force of a soon-to-be seventeen-year-old girl's rage, even it can break.

"I don't want to be a fucking actress, you stupid fucking cow!" Cordelia screamed at her mother and used her now empty hands to first slam them down on the table so hard that the remaining unbroken dishes clattered, and then she pushed herself up from the table. "You have two other understudies waiting in the wings sitting right there," Cordelia violently pointed at fifteen-year-old Miranda and twelve-year-old Portia. "I'm not talentless and neurotic like you, Mother, so I could actually do something or become someone that really fucking matters!"

All those still seated at the dining table had witnessed her silent pouting for years, but none had ever seen her throw a temper tantrum, nor had any of them ever heard her raise her voice or use profanity, sans the occasional 'bloody.' Her sisters wore the expressions of girls who now realized they would no longer be able to bully their older sister. Her father was rendered speechless by not only her language but also by the vehemence with which it was spoken.

Beatrice, however, was not the least bit surprised that deep down in the depths of Cordelia's very essence, hidden behind the solemnity and fastidiousness, lay a passionate and unbridled person waiting to be unleashed. For the past three weeks, that's exactly who she'd been trying to awaken each time she criticized Cordelia's posture, rigidity, elocution, awkwardness, and virginity.

Beatrice was ecstatic that she'd been called a 'stupid fucking cow' by her eldest daughter. Yet, she knew that she couldn't show it—yes, Cordelia was painfully oblivious to verbal and visual cues, but she wasn't stupid, either.

Instead of jovially shouting, '*I knew you had more than probiotics running through your veins*,' Beatrice stared directly at and through her daughter and, in a controlled, almost apathetic voice, said, "No one is more 'neurotic' than you, Darling. As for the 'talentless' bit, we will work on that tomorrow morning, beginning at nine. Now, you are excused to go to your sterilization chamber… Oh, and on your way, please ask Mrs. Holt how much I should take out of your wages for that plate you smashed."

* * *

The first year and a half of Cordelia's apprenticeship at the Wainwright was, to say the very least, tempestuous. Mother and daughter fought constantly, not only at the theater but also at home. While Beatrice had longed to unleash her daughter's inner passion, she was not prepared for it to be directed at her quite so viciously.

For someone who'd never spoken profanity before her outburst at the family dining table, Cordelia developed a proficiency with it that would've made members of the Royal Navy blush. There was nothing she wouldn't say when she got angry at her mother for refusing to end her training and allow her to go to college to study economics.

While personal verbal assaults were mainly reserved for home—good English breeding would not allow Cordelia to refer to Beatrice as a 'fucking: bitch; bint; cow; minger; blighter; and git' in front of anyone at the theater—she had no qualms about bellowing 'Goddammit to bloody fucking hell' whenever her mother or any of the other players commented on her inability to remember her lines, cues, or standing positions whenever she was forced to stand in for someone at rehearsal.

At one particular rehearsal of *The Winter's Tale*, she'd had to stand in as Perdita for a young actress who'd come down with food poisoning. This was most unfortunate because the company was running lines for *Act IV, Scene IV*, where Perdita has some of her most extended lines in the play.

Typically, it was perfectly acceptable for stand-ins, especially first-year apprentices, to keep a script ready if needed. Cordelia rarely did this because of her surface dyslexia, making it extremely difficult for her to read words aloud directly off a page. This is why her *preferred* method of learning was auditory, namely audiobooks. The problem was that only she and her mother knew that she suffered from this *affliction*.

So, when yet again Cordelia didn't know her lines and the conceited prick playing Florizel screamed at her, "Why don't you read from the bloody script, you ingrate!" she soundly smacked him across the face and stormed off the *so, so, so solid* wood stage screaming, "Goddammit to bloody fucking hell."

All hell broke loose when Beatrice found her hiding in Henry's office.

"Goddammit, Delia! You cannot physically batter members of this company. Do you want us to get sued?" Beatrice yelled as she slammed the door shut.

"Yes, I hope that jackhole takes this fucking theater for every pound it has. That way, I won't have to fucking be here anymore!"

Beatrice looked at her daughter as though she were the one who'd been slapped. "You ungrateful little bitch. This theater pays for our house, the depressing clothes on your back, and your sisters' outrageously priced schooling—not to mention all the other people at this company who depend on it for a living for themselves and their families."

"At least I am a realistic little bitch, Mother, unlike you. In what world am I *ever* going to be able to remember all those goddamn lines with my damaged brain?" Cordelia pleaded with her mother.

Beatrice was not unsympathetic to Cordelia's plight. Still, she wasn't willing to let her daughter use it as an excuse to escape to an uneventful, lonely, and sterile world filled with numbers, solitude, and disinfectants.

Cordelia went nowhere other than to the theater and her *fortress of cleanliness*—her room, where Beatrice suspected she spent her time listening to audiobooks about disease instead of the complete works of Shakespeare. She had no friends, and she certainly had no boyfriends. No matter how much black Cordelia wore or how little makeup she refused to wear, she was still a stunningly beautiful young woman. She may have had the personality of flat, black paint, but her looks alone were enough to attract horny men of all ages. Cordelia was utterly oblivious—or, as Beatrice reckoned, repulsed by the idea of anyone putting their germ-infested hands on her.

When Beatrice once spied her daughter staring intently at the shapely legs of one of the younger female players, she was overcome with relief that her daughter showed signs of not being an automaton devoid of all human desire. Yet, when she'd given her daughter a vibrator for her eighteenth birthday and suggested that she might think of those same legs when she used it, Cordelia looked at her as though she were speaking a foreign language.

With these things in mind, Beatrice addressed Cordelia's actual *affliction*.

"It isn't your difficulty with the written word that makes you 'damaged,' Darling. It is your unequivocal refusal to acknowledge how you feel about other people—that is, besides your blind hatred of me.

"You are undoubtedly the most miserable person I have encountered in my entire life—and I have worked with some of the most self-loathing performers to walk across the stage. You cannot live your life as though you reside inside some sterilized bubble floating across the sea because one day that bubble is going to burst, and you will be drowned because you have no idea how to function outside of it.

"Your father and I don't care if you fancy boys or *girls*; we just want you to show interest in something other than bloody germs."

Cordelia's response to her mother's heartfelt entreaty was, "I have absolutely no fucking idea to what you are referring. I just want to be left alone and not to have to come to this goddamn torture chamber every fucking day for the rest of my 'miserable' life."

"Yes, Darling, you have made it abundantly clear that is what you would *prefer*."

That is precisely why Beatrice made Cordelia come to the theater every day.

CHAPTER SIX

"The Virgin of St. Albans"

Dec. 1998-Jan. 1999: St. Albans, England

England has a long and storied affection for primogeniture, whereby property and titles are passed down to the eldest son, no matter how many sisters may have preceded said son in birth. The most famous example of this practice was King Henry VIII's two daughters, Mary and Elizabeth, being denied, albeit only temporarily, the throne in favor of their younger and most ineffectual brother, Edward. Anne Boleyn losing her head and the English Reformation were direct results of this patriarchal need for a male heir to carry on the legacy of a family's name.

The Wainwright family subscribed to this practice in theory only. The family theater opened its Mayfair doors to the public in 1853, and, while it was *preferable* to keep the ownership of it in male hands, there were instances, mainly due to wars, epidemics, and/or latent homosexuality, that ownership fell inadvertently into the delicate hands of the eldest Wainwright female.

Since English Common Law didn't require a married woman to take her husband's surname, most Wainwright women kept their own. This is why Cordelia's mother was Beatrice Wainwright and not Beatrice Highsmith and her three daughters also carried the Wainwright name, especially since she had no son to pass it along to.

Most Wainwright women were actresses, although some less attractive ones found themselves backstage mending costumes, painting scenery, or worse, out front checking coats, serving refreshments, and/or selling tickets. Some of the actresses married other actors, but many, like Beatrice, wed men with backgrounds in business who could take over management of the theater if needed. This is what happened to Henry Highsmith when his father-in-law, Antony Wainwright, died of a massive coronary at age fifty-eight.

After graduating from Cambridge University with a degree in economics, Henry worked for Lloyds Banking Group as a financial analyst. He met Beatrice soon after that, and they were married in 1978—he was twenty-five, and she was a mere nineteen.

Two Junes later, they had their first daughter, Cordelia. One year later, Beatrice was expecting Miranda, and his father-in-law unceremoniously keeled over in the office that Henry was forced to take over at the age of twenty-eight. He had no idea how to run a theater, let alone how one produced Shakespearean plays, so he hired Geoffrey Abbott as the Wainwright's in-house producer.

This was also why Henry deferred to his wife regarding his daughters' chosen profession. So, while he felt profound sympathy for Cordelia's apparent desire to be anything other than an actress, he mostly sat silently by and watched Beatrice force his painfully shy and awkward daughter into a spotlight she so *desperately* wanted to escape.

For nearly two exceedingly long years of the War of the Wainwrights, he listened to mother and daughter mercilessly verbally assault one another. Cordelia had been such a quiet but somewhat eccentric child, who spent most of her summers with him in the theater's office. She kept the office clean and tidy and asked questions about projected revenues. This is why her transformation into a profanity-screaming, foot-stomping, hand-and-door-slamming teenager was so shocking to him.

On the very rare occasion that he dared to say to his wife, "Perhaps she would be better suited working with me in the office, Sweetheart," Beatrice would dismiss him and say, "That is the absolute worst place for that girl to end up, Henry! Do you want her to become some godforsaken spinster cat-lady who spends her days crunching numbers and her nights deep-cleaning her house?" Her determined, intransigent tone was the only reason that he didn't remind her that their daughter would never own an animal that shed.

Henry often wished Cordelia would just run away from the life she was being forced to lead. Unfortunately, she had neither the financial means nor the emotional fortitude to do so. Cordelia's small trust could not be remitted until she turned twenty-one, and he couldn't see her taking a menial job, where she would no doubt have to interact with other people to earn a living. And, God forbid, if she were forced to live in some filthy hostel with oversexed people her own age, she might quite literally kill herself—*probably with pills because the sight of blood makes her nauseous.*

This is why when Christmastime arrived, it was his fervent wish that there be no talk of the Wainwright, which closed for three weeks every year for the holidays. He didn't often make demands on Beatrice, but he told her in no uncertain terms that *all* of the Wainwrights needed a break from the constant domestic discord and made her swear not to mention the theater, acting, and/or Shakespeare in their eldest daughter's presence. Additionally, no one was to attempt to force Cordelia to go watch a pantomime in town or to wear a red or green jumper with a reindeer on it. She was to be left alone to do whatever she pleased.

For three glorious weeks, Cordelia stayed in her room and did absolutely nothing but sleep and watch the BBC miniseries *The Human Body.* Beatrice was convinced that her daughter only joined the family each night for dinner because she knew Mrs. Holt was serving various Christmas puddings. There she sat in complete silence—no profanity was spewed, no voices were raised, and no expensive china was broken. It irritated Beatrice to no end.

Beatrice was entirely bewildered that a beautiful eighteen-year-old girl wasn't out every night with friends at the pub or seeing a film with a boyfriend or a girlfriend. Of course, Cordelia had made no friends at St. Mary's except some depressing girl named Sloane, and she certainly hadn't made any at the theater with her volatile personality. As for finding a possible romantic partner, that appeared to be the furthest thing from her daughter's mind. She was so unlike her sister, Miranda, who had two boyfriends simultaneously.

It's just not normal, Beatrice constantly said to herself.

When she broached the subject with Henry, he joked, "You are way *too* young to become a grandmother, Sweetheart." His wife was only thirty-nine.

"I don't think that'll be an issue, Dear. If Delia has *any* predilections, I suspect they would be towards the fairer sex."

Beatrice had noticed several times that her daughter was particularly preoccupied with the long, shapely legs of a young, dark-haired woman named Kate, who'd joined the Wainwright the previous spring.

"You don't say…Well, perhaps Delia is reluctant to tell us she has a girlfriend. You should—"

Beatrice irritably cut him off, "I *already* have, Henry! Last summer, I told her we didn't care about that sort of thing. The issue is that she doesn't care about that sort of thing *at all*. That thing I bought her for her birthday is still in its goddamn box—sealed shut! What eighteen-year-old girl has no…*urges*? It's just not normal. I think we need to take Delia to see someone."

Henry was far past embarrassed by this conversation. "Can't you just suggest to Dr. Stewart that she address…*this*…in her next session?" Cordelia had been seeing a psychiatrist for years for her preoccupation with germs and cleanliness.

"I'm not talking about that type of *professional* help, Dear," Beatrice clarified.

He felt as if his head might explode. "Beatrice!"

"Don't be such a prude, Henry. Men do it all the time. In France, it's practically a rite of passage for a father to take his son to a bordello."

She's lost her bloody mind, Henry thought. "Can you really see our daughter willingly going into such an establishment? The same girl who changes her bedsheets every other day—and only every other day because she was explicitly told not to do it daily? My God, Beatrice! You're as crazy as she is!"

The instant he said this, he was ashamed of himself. It was an unspoken rule between wife and husband to never refer to Cordelia as 'crazy'—odd, peculiar, and different were the acceptable adjectives.

"She's not crazy!" Beatrice yelled furiously. "She's...*peculiar* and surely frustrated—or at least her poor body must be by this point. No one can *always* be so bloody angry because they think they don't want to be an actress. I'm just about at the end of my rope, Henry, with all of her rage being directed squarely at me," she said in a defeated tone.

He couldn't believe it when he said it. "She likes watching documentaries, so why don't you go back to *that* place and buy her some...videos?"

* * *

When rehearsals for *The Tempest* resumed the second week of January, Beatrice noticed a marked improvement in Cordelia's mood. Gone were the tantrums and the yelling. When she'd been told that she would be the understudy to Kate for the part of Iris, Cordelia only slightly raised her voice when she said, "But I'm not ready, Mother!"

Beatrice attributed this personality shift to the black gift box she'd discreetly left on her daughter's bed containing three videos, the unopened vibrator, a slew of AA batteries, bottles of Astro Glide and Purell, and a handwritten note:

These are for you, Darling. We need never speak of this, but if you have one ounce of love left in your heart for your mother, please use them. You may never thank me, but I'm quite certain that your poor body will.
Love,
Mummy

To cover all of her bases, Beatrice told the shopgirl that the videos should be "instructional, with a variety of persuasions, but nothing too overwhelmingly dirty—her mind is the only thing she hasn't tried to disinfect *yet*."

For the next three months, everyone at the theater and in the Wainwright household—most especially her mother—much *preferred* the new and improved version of Cordelia Wainwright.

CHAPTER SEVEN

"A Tragedy of Repression"

Jan.-Feb. 1999: London & St. Albans, England

There are many splendid things that a person experiences when they make the giant leap from adolescence into adulthood, such as independence and romantic love. Yet, as with everything in life, there are also downsides to adult actualization, such as dependency and heartbreak. The difference between a healthy adult and an unhealthy one is how a person deals with their successes and, more importantly, their failures.

As a somewhat well-adjusted adult herself, Beatrice knew these were lessons that Cordelia must learn for herself if she were ever to live some semblance of a happy, normal life. While she was immeasurably pleased with the yielded results of the discreet black box she'd left on her daughter's bed, Beatrice was also aware that the greatest gift she could give Cordelia was freedom—and, in the event of its downside, her love and guidance.

* * *

While no one openly discussed why Cordelia was so preoccupied with germs and cleanliness, everyone knew it stemmed directly from Beatrice's younger sister, Jessica's death at the very young age of twenty-five.

On the last night of the company's spring production of *Hamlet*, where she had performed as Ophelia, Jessica gashed her arm on a rusty nail that had come loose from a doorframe. She'd been quickly patched up between *Act II* and *Act III*, and the show went on without a hitch.

A week-and-a-half later, having not heard from her sister who, unlike herself, lived in town, Beatrice went to check on Jessica after taking eight-year-old Cordelia to see the pediatrician. When there was no answer at the door, a concerned Beatrice asked the building manager to let her into the flat. The entire apartment smelled like putrid vomit and spoiled food; the sink was full of unwashed dishes, and half-empty takeout cartons littered the countertops. They found Jessica lying unconscious in bed, burning up with fever and an unsightly infected wound on her left arm. Three days later, she died in hospital from sepsis brought on by untreated tetanus.

Had Beatrice known that a simple case of hay fever could lead to a lifetime phobia of bacterial infection, she would have made Cordelia drink an entire bottle of children's Benadryl and then happily called Social Services on herself. Instead, Beatrice had to take her traumatized daughter to see a psychiatrist.

To combat her patient's depression, anxiety, and unnatural obsession with germs and cleanliness, Dr. Stewart first prescribed Prozac for Cordelia when she was just twelve years old. Cordelia's dosage started at 10mg, and by the age of eighteen, she was taking 60mg per day. Like any good Brit, Beatrice *preferred* to calm her nerves with a Gordon's gin and tonic, but polite society frowned upon serving hard liquor to minors. So, she reluctantly agreed to put Cordelia on a drug that made her even more depressed and anxious than she already was.

Additionally, because of the high dosage that Cordelia took, the consumption of alcohol was strongly discouraged. So, when she turned eighteen, there was no trip to the pub to have her first legal drink, and when the other young people at the company invited her out for drinks after rehearsal—that is, after she began acting somewhat normal—she politely declined. Beatrice was quite certain that it wasn't only the Prozac that prevented her daughter from socializing with her peers, but it was still a barrier nonetheless.

"Not everyone who goes to the pub drinks, Delia. Just have a Coke," Beatrice suggested.

"What if they ask why I do not drink? They all think I am crazy already, Mother."

"Don't say that!" Beatrice said sharply. *God, I hate that word!* "Tell them you're on antibiotics; they'd definitely believe *that*."

Even Cordelia found the humor in her mother's witty dig, but there were other obstacles to her going. "But how will I get home?"

"In a bloody taxi!" Beatrice exasperatedly said. Then, she saw the look of horror on Cordelia's face. "Yes, I know, Darling, it's probably filled with all sorts of possible pathogens, but since you refuse to learn how to drive, sooner or later, you're going to have to use public transportation. Mummy can't drive you everywhere for the rest of your life, you know."

Much to Beatrice's surprise, Cordelia agreed. And, so, with a pack of Clorox disinfectant wipes in her purse, she went to the pub for nearly two hours, drank three Cokes, rode home in a taxi with the window down, and then took an excessively long shower. It was a start.

* * *

While Beatrice could ever-so-gently push her fledgling out of the nest when it came to socializing with people outside her own bloodline, she could not so easily protect her from the impending sharp talons of heartbreak she saw coming every day at the theater.

Though Cordelia would never admit it, probably even to herself, Beatrice knew her daughter was infatuated with the young woman she was understudying, Kate. When Geoffrey suggested the idea, Beatrice had doubts—not because Cordelia wasn't prepared to be more than a rehearsal stand-in, but because she knew her daughter wasn't ready to have her heart broken.

Kate was an attractive twenty-two-year-old brunette who wore tight, short skirts that showed off a pair of long legs and a firm, round ass that would make Jennifer Lopez jealous. Every day at rehearsal, Beatrice would watch as her daughter hung on every word out of Kate's pouty lips and how her eyes would slowly work their way up from the floorboards to that firm ass and then back down to the boards. It took all of Beatrice's restraint not to ask Cordelia if she needed a handkerchief to wipe away her drool.

While she was pleased that Cordelia's videos had obviously awakened her dormant libido, Beatrice greatly wished that they had also instructed her on how to identify women who were interested in helping her satisfy it because Kate certainly didn't belong in that category.

Kate was a notorious slag who'd slept with just about every straight man in their company in less than a year—including Geoffrey, who'd brought her into the theater because of it. As usual, when it came to matters of sex, Cordelia was unequivocally clueless and had no idea that the object of her desire was the company's in-house whore.

Though she was doubtful that Cordelia was quite ready to act on her feelings of lust, Beatrice wasn't willing to take a chance on those feelings being rejected by the likes of such a tart. And, much like King Duncan's fateful decision to kill Cawdor in *Macbeth*, Beatrice made her own immoral, fateful decision to have Geoffrey sack Kate, thus setting off a series of unfortunate events that ended in, well, Shakespearean tragedy.

It would be an understatement to say that Kate didn't take her firing well. Much like her namesake in *The Taming of the Shrew*, she had a quick temper and an even sharper tongue. Once Geoffrey had privately dealt the blow, she proceeded not to the exit but to the stage, where the entire company was running lines, and confronted Beatrice.

"How dare you sack me so that you can put your pathetic daughter up on the stage!"

Usually on cue, Beatrice was utterly unprepared for this reaction. Every pair of eyes was pointed directly at her, but the two she was most concerned with were Cordelia's icy-blue ones, who looked at her mother as though she'd betrayed her in the worst possible manner.

"*That* is not why you were sacked. Your less-than-professional behavior is why your services are no longer needed at this company."

"Oh, so I'm to be sacked because I shagged a few blokes, is it? That seems like a bit of a double standard—or are they to be sacked, too? Starting with fucking Geoffrey?"

As the theater's finances were precarious at best, Beatrice didn't want this, well, *shrew*, running to a solicitor or, God forbid, the Department for Work and Pensions, so she had to choose her words carefully.

"No one cares whom you do or do not sleep with, but when it affects the overall morale of this company and creates discord, you leave us with no other solution."

"Hmm…are you sure about that—not caring about whom I sleep with?" Kate asked with venom practically dripping from her lips. She then turned like a viper and slithered towards Cordelia. "Or is it that you don't want me to fuck Sappho over here. You don't think I see how you leer at me? You'd like to have a go at me in the costume room, wouldn't you?"

For once in her life, Cordelia was not rendered speechless. "I take enough pills from the chemist; I have no desire to add Ceftriaxone to the list." Then, she walked directly off the *so, so, so solid* wood stage, as the entire company burst into laughter.

* * *

Beatrice found her daughter in Henry's office, sitting silently at his *hideous* black, gold-inlaid pigeon-hole desk, wearing headphones and scribbling notes into her Letts' planner with her father's *ridiculous* Conway Stewart fountain pen. As she stood there watching Cordelia, trying to gather her thoughts about how to explain her actions, Beatrice could not have envisioned how many variations of this scene would play out in Cordelia's life.

When she sat beside Cordelia, she saw an empty glass that held the amber remnants of what she rightly assumed was from the flask of Jameson that Henry kept in the center drawer of his desk. She motioned for her daughter to remove her headphones and then struggled with her words. "Delia…"

With her best stage smile, Cordelia rescued her mother's lack of words with her own. "Do not fret, Mother. I am fully prepared to assume the role of Iris. You have taught me all the *lessons* I need to be a successful *actress*. Thank you. Now, if you do not mind, I would *prefer* to return to studying my cues and lines." She then slid the headphones back onto her ears, tilted her head toward the desk, and returned to scribbling.

Had Beatrice known that a simple case of teenage heartbreak could lead to a decade of sexual repression, she would have allowed her daughter to eventually be humiliated by her unrequited desires. Instead, Beatrice silently watched her daughter vehemently disavow any romantic entanglement—unrequited or welcomed: *I would have much preferred heartbreak.*

CHAPTER EIGHT

"Mother's Labour's Lost"

March 1999: London & St. Albans, England

At 2,039 lines, *The Tempest* is the second shortest play in the Shakespearean canon. Of those 2,039 lines, Cordelia only needed to recite four of them as Iris in the first scene of *Act IV*. The issue wasn't that three of those four lines were exceptionally long—she'd mastered the art of memorization by this point in her training—but that once her last line was mercifully uttered, she had to perform a carefully choreographed intricate dance with two other female players.

Cordelia, unsurprisingly, didn't know how to dance by herself, let alone with two other people in unison, while wearing a pair of *fucking* fairy wings. Night after endless night, she stumbled and fumbled across the *so, so, so solid* wood stage. And, night after endless night, there was unmistakable laughter from the audience.

This was humiliating enough, but because she was a Wainwright making her stage debut, every critic in England wrote about it in their bloody newspaper columns. These 'reviews,' which to their undeserved credit mentioned her stunning good looks, effortless delivery, and graceless dancing abilities, filled the cheap seats of the theater with not only train wreck aficionados but one very expensive balcony seat—a seat that Beatrice later had removed and burned.

* * *

"I thought you did much better tonight, Darling," Beatrice said comfortingly to Cordelia, watching her daughters remove their stage makeup in her dressing room mirror.

Delia's eyes look a bit glassy.

Miranda, now seventeen, had joined the theater and been put to work almost immediately because, unlike her older sister, she'd performed in numerous theatrical productions at St. Mary's. Her principal role in *The Tempest* was to ensure that Cordelia didn't trip over her feet.

As was her custom, Beatrice had taken the season's first show off to concentrate on her role as Gertrude in *Hamlet*, which was always the second spring season show at the Wainwright. This year, it was an especially prudent decision, as it gave her ample time to focus on Cordelia's fraught debut and nerves—namely, she had to nightly hold her daughter's hair back from her face as she threw up.

"Yes, Delia, you only stumbled twice tonight," Miranda unhelpfully added. When she saw her mother staring daggers behind her in the mirror, she pushed down any giggles that might unwisely escape.

"Must I wear these fucking wings, Mother?" Cordelia asked as she ripped said wings from her back and threw them unceremoniously across the room.

This question was asked after every performance, and every night, Beatrice would shake her head in exasperation and retrieve the wayward wings that had flown across the room.

"You're playing a fairy nymph, Delia, so—" but before she could finish saying 'yes,' there was a knock at the door.

When she opened it, she almost slammed it shut immediately.

"This is Mayfair, so if you've come looking for Judi, take a ten-minute ride on the Tube to Waterloo, and I'm sure you'll find her there."

Both sisters immediately stopped removing their makeup when they heard their mother's tone. That tone was reserved for people their mother despised, like Tony Blair and Ms. Akers, the culinary-challenged young woman who filled in as the family's cook whenever Mrs. Holt went on holiday.

"Ah, Beatrice, I've missed that acerbic wit of yours. I was wondering if I might have a word with your daughter?" asked a posh-sounding male voice.

"Miranda's even too young for the likes of you, Grant!" Beatrice said menacingly.

This elicited a deep chuckle from the mystery man at the door. "No, the other one, Ms. Pavlova."

This request was not quite as frightening to Beatrice as the idea of Miranda being bedded by a forty-five-year-old sleazebag. He didn't stand a chance in hell with Cordelia, for obvious reasons, but also because he wore an inordinate amount of Polo cologne and, worse, a beard. So, she stood aside and let him in.

"Girls, this is Grant Andrews."

The girls didn't need their mother to introduce him. Grant Andrews, a well-known director and producer, made modern-day film adaptations of classic books and plays. Their mother referred to him as 'The Butcher' because of his complete irreverence for the great works of literature he 'shoved down the meat grinder of good taste.' He was average looking at best, with obviously dyed jet-black hair, smarmy green eyes, and a crooked smile filled with capped and bleached teeth. Worse, he was wearing a black Armani suit—their father had told them to never trust an Englishman who wore an Italian suit.

When Cordelia didn't stand to introduce herself, he smiled at Beatrice. "I see the apple doesn't fall far from the tree.

"Right, I saw your *performance* tonight. You're obviously not a dancer, but you have a pleasant-sounding voice, good, though a bit relaxed, posture, and a face that the camera will absolutely love—not to mention you're quite fit. I'm looking for a fresh, new face to fill the now-vacant role of Ophelia in my next film. Would you be interested in doing a screen test?"

Beatrice sharply answered for her daughter, "Over my dead body! No daughter of mine will work on one of your vulgar productions—especially not on what I can only assume will be a complete abomination of *Hamlet*. And, why on Earth would you want to do *Hamlet*? Didn't Branagh just make a far superior adaptation to anything you could *ever* dream of making?"

"Yes, and he lost millions of pounds. My version is more modern and will appeal to a much wider audience," Grant explained.

"I bet it will!" Beatrice said with derision in her voice. She then whipped the door open and pointed him toward the exit. "But you'll have to sell your rubbish without my daughter's assistance. Now, get the fuck out of my dressing room!"

Neither sister had ever heard their mother say 'fuck,' so this alone was shocking, but they were even more surprised by her unabashed detestation of him.

Grant was the type of man who always wanted the last word, so instead of following Beatrice's pointed finger out the door, he reached inside his expensive Italian suit, pulled out a card, and walked over to a speechless Cordelia.

"Call me when this gets *old*."

When he said 'old,' he made it a point to look directly at Beatrice, who was still waiting to slam the door shut behind him. Then he dropped the card in Cordelia's lap, winked, spun around in his Italian loafers, and walked out the door without a word to Beatrice—who promptly slammed the door behind him.

When Beatrice turned around to look at her daughters, she didn't like what she saw. Cordelia held *that man's* card like a Willy Wonka Golden Ticket.

"Cordelia Anne Wainwright, if you know what's good for you, you'll burn that card like it's covered in Plague. He doesn't give out roles to young actresses for free!"

"Yes, Mother."

* * *

This is the thing about anxiety, such as being excessively worried about germs and bacteria; it can manifest itself into other forms of anxiety. A person can become obsessive regarding cleanliness, order, and time. That same person can also exhibit depressive symptoms such as fatigue, anti-social behavior, moodiness, and a reduced sex drive. And, if that same individual has a profession that requires them to speak in front of others, it can lead to stage fright.

Stage fright can present itself in many ways, both emotionally and physically. For example, one might experience throat tightness, cottonmouth, nausea, and an extreme case of paranoia and fear of rejection. These are the symptoms that Cordelia encountered every night of her month-long run of *The Tempest*. The fact that she had to wait nearly one hundred minutes every night to go on stage in *Act IV* only exacerbated the situation.

To cope, she took a healthy swig of cheap vodka from a flask that she kept in her purse at the start of each of the first three acts and a second 60mg Prozac at the beginning of *Act II*. At best, she weighed 110 lbs. soaking wet, and her stomach was usually empty by *Act II* because she'd vomited what little food she could choke down that particular day. By the time she went on stage in *Act IV* to say her four lines and perform that *stupid* dance, she was high as a kite.

It was a miracle that she could remember her name, let alone her lines, but somehow she managed it. Yet, it's one thing to stand in place to deliver lines you've seared into your brain via audio recordings and quite another to perform an intricate dance sequence with two other people. How she did it for so long without falling flat on her face only God knows; but, on the second to last show of *The Tempest*'s run, she not only fell flat on her face, but her head hit the *so, so, so solid* wood stage of the Wainwright so soundly that she was knocked unconscious.

When she woke up in a bed in the Accident and Emergency room, she felt as though she'd been run over by a lorry. Then, she had to deal with her mother—given the choice, she would've chosen the lorry any day.

"What were you thinking! And don't you dare say you tripped over your own goddamn feet! They did blood work! I knew your eyes looked glassy—and not even you could be that clumsy of a dancer!" Beatrice's yelling could be heard by everyone in the A&E. "These *people* asked me if you needed a referral for bloody *rehab!*"

Cordelia's only response to this tirade was to lean over the side of the bed and unceremoniously vomit.

Having heard Beatrice's berating of her concussed daughter, the A&E doctors took pity on Cordelia and kept her overnight in the hospital and gently suggested that Beatrice might go home and then collect Cordelia the next day.

The idea of staying overnight in a place where sickness and bacteria lurked around every corner never sounded better to Cordelia.

* * *

Henry was the one who came to collect Cordelia the next day. This decision was twofold. One, his wife was still livid with their eldest daughter's 'absolute stupidity.' Two, as there was yet one more performance of *The Tempest* left, Beatrice had to prepare their middle daughter, Miranda, to step in as Cordelia's replacement.

These reasons for her mother's absence were particularly hurtful to Cordelia. No, she did not wish to have a repeat 'conversation' with Beatrice about how she'd ended up in the hospital in the first place. Still, Beatrice's indifference as to why Cordelia overmedicated was upsetting.

As puzzling as it was, especially with how much they'd previously argued with one another about Cordelia becoming an actress, the first three months of 1999 found mother and daughter getting on rather amicably. Their newfound mother-daughter bond was the direct result of Cordelia's newfound discovery of her clitoris and the realization that she actually liked acting. Cordelia had her mother to thank for both.

Though her role as Iris was small, it gave her something to focus on at the theater other than how an actress stands, speaks, and moves about the stage. While mechanics are essential tools in an actress' tool-belt, what most intrigued Cordelia about the craft of acting was first understanding and then becoming the character she was to portray—it allowed her to be someone entirely different than herself.

In *The Tempest*, Iris is ethereal, beautiful, and exudes a radiant aura. Yes, Cordelia was an attractive young woman, but no one would ever describe her as radiant—especially her personality—and the only delicate thing about her was her mental state. Yet, for approximately ten minutes every night, she pretended to be all those things—and she loved it.

But she didn't love that she had to do it in front of a live audience. She did exceedingly well at rehearsals with her mother and other company members watching because she knew them and, for the most part, they were encouraging. A live audience was an entirely different matter—especially once their unkind laughter at her woeful dancing skills began.

Cordelia didn't like to be judged, which is difficult to overcome when performing live in front of people who come to the theater to do just that. That is why she, much like Prospero, who employed magic to perform illusions in *The Tempest*, used vodka and an extra Prozac to conjure up the courage to go on stage every night to be judged.

Then, there was the humiliation of having her younger sister, Miranda, take over her role. Yes, it was only for one night, but Cordelia was already jealous enough of her sister, who was what she couldn't be herself—normal.

Miranda had a sparkling personality that people gravitated toward, and she enjoyed being the center of attention. She had gobs of friends and, most obnoxiously, boyfriends.

Whenever Cordelia had to ride alone with her to the theater, Miranda wasn't shy about telling her older sister *exactly* what she did with them, either: "I thought my head was going to explode when he put his tongue between my legs. You should get yourself a girlfriend, Delia—you'd like it very much, and it would definitely relax you and might help with your nerves about going on stage."

Delia was confident she'd like it, too, but was just as positive that it would never happen. Instead, she would have to live vicariously, though very unwantedly, through Miranda's stories of her own sexual exploits—thankfully, Portia was only fourteen, so Cordelia would be spared the indignity of both her younger sisters explicitly describing their orgasms to her for another four years.

When she asked Henry if they could stop by the Wainwright on their way home from the hospital, he didn't look at her but quietly said, "You need your rest."

What he didn't say is that his wife had instructed him to take Cordelia directly home and lock her in her 'sterilization chamber'—it needed to be tidied up because Beatrice had spent the night before going over Cordelia's room like a drug dog, searching for hidden pills and drink. In the morning, before leaving for the theater, she'd told Mrs. Holt to lock up all the liquor in the house, called to sack Dr. Stewart, and threatened to sue her for malpractice.

So, Cordelia had to wait all day and evening to be told what the Fates—Beatrice—had decided to do with her. At 11:15 p.m., her bedroom door flew open without a knock, and her mother pronounced judgment: "You will go with your father to the office from now on."

"But, Mother…" Cordelia stammered, sitting up in bed.

Beatrice cut her off with a severe arm swipe through the air— her version of the Sword of Damocles. "No buts, Delia! You are obviously not cut out for the stage. I should've listened to you when you said you wanted to be a number cruncher. Now, look what I have turned you into! You could've killed yourself last night!" Her anguished words were filled with regret.

"I'm sure I can…" Cordelia anxiously tried to reason with her mother.

But Beatrice didn't want to hear it.

"You can what? Become a drunk and drug addict by the age of twenty? I love you too much to let that happen, Darling."

With that, she kissed her daughter on the forehead, dejectedly walked to the door, and shut down Cordelia's hopes of escaping herself.

* * *

Apr. 8, 1999: London & St. Albans, England

Here's the thing about being told you can't do what you most want to do: it makes you want to do it even more—especially soon-to-be nineteen-year-old girls.

For a week, Cordelia went to the theater office every day with her father and crunched numbers while Beatrice and Miranda were on stage preparing for the company's opening night performance of *Hamlet*. Miranda had been named the understudy for the role of Ophelia.

Just as her mother had been born to play Lady Macbeth, Cordelia was most assuredly born to play the role of a depressed young maiden driven mad by unrequited love. It was unbearable to hear Miranda incessantly prattle on about how much she hoped Jenny, the young actress she was understudying, came down with some malady that prevented her from performing.

So, on opening night, Cordelia made the decision that shaped the next eighteen years of her adult life. She asked Miranda to borrow one of her dresses and had Portia help her apply makeup to her face. She then went with Henry and Portia to the theater and knocked on her mother's dressing room door.

"I just wanted to wish you good luck this evening, Mother," she said as she entered the room.

"Goddamnit, Delia, you know that's bad luck! You say 'break a leg,'" Beatrice chided her daughter. But when she looked back at Cordelia in the dressing mirror, she didn't see *Delia*. No, what she saw was an entirely different person.

Gone were the black jeans, the black The Cure T-shirt, and the black trainers. Instead, Cordelia wore a black gabardine sheath dress cut above her knees, with three-quarter sleeves, an asymmetrical draped neckline, a banded waist with a slim belt, and three-inch black heels. Her strawberry-blond hair was pulled up into a French twist, and she had on makeup.

Alarm bells immediately went off—just ten minutes before the curtain went up.

Beatrice slowly turned around in her chair to better look at her daughter—not the outfit. "You look *different*, Darling…Perhaps I should tell you not to break a leg."

"Do I?" Cordelia nervously asked, smoothing down an imperceptible wrinkle on the dress. "I thought I'd try something *different* tonight."

Second alarm bell: using a contraction—Cordelia had a tell.

"How *different*?" Beatrice worriedly asked as she stood and walked to where her daughter was standing by the door. She wanted to see those icy-blue eyes up close.

As her mother drew nearer, Cordelia awkwardly brushed back a stray hair from her face and tilted her head slightly to the side to avert Beatrice's fierce gaze. "I thought you'd be happy to see me—"

Beatrice cut Cordelia off by grabbing her daughter's chin with her right hand and repositioning it so she could look directly into her eyes. "Oh, I *see* you, Darling. I see a girl standing on the precipice of womanhood who wants her mother's permission to… *Do*…whatever she thinks she must do to attain it. Am I right?"

"Mother, I don't know what—" Cordelia said, attempting to side-step her mother's pointed question, but Beatrice's grip on her chin tightened.

Beatrice's blue eyes bore down into her daughter's wide eyes, imploring her to heed every word she was about to say. "I love you, Darling, but I will not give it. I have done my best to teach you right from wrong, and now you must decide for yourself."

She then released her grip from Cordelia's chin, used the same hand to brush back the hair around her forehead, and placed a kiss there. Then she walked out the door without another word.

* * *

Hamlet is the longest play in the Shakespearean canon at 3,728 lines. The Wainwright production ran three hours and fifteen minutes, with two fifteen-minute intermissions. Of those 3,728 lines, Beatrice had to speak sixty-nine of them over the entirety of the five-act play. In between acts, she would look into the audience to see if Cordelia was seated beside Henry and Portia, but she was not.

The play started at 7:00 p.m. and ended at approximately 10:45 p.m. With it being opening night, Beatrice was obligated to have a celebratory drink with the cast afterward, which lasted another thirty minutes. Driving from Mayfair back home to St. Albans took another twenty minutes.

When she arrived home at approximately midnight, Beatrice went straight to Cordelia's room. As she entered, she could hear the shower running in the adjoining bathroom, and she sat on Cordelia's bed and waited. The instant she saw her daughter slide open the bathroom door, she knew Cordelia had made the wrong decision.

Cordelia, whose head and body were wrapped in white towels, was startled to find her mother waiting for her but tried to act like she wasn't.

"Did the show go well, then, Mother?"

"How much soap did you have to use?" Beatrice asked in a steely voice.

"Well, you know me, Mother, I like to be clean," Cordelia attempted to joke.

"After what I suspect you've done tonight, you will never be clean again! You stupid girl!" Beatrice yelled.

"Mother, I—" Cordelia began, but Beatrice quickly stood up from the bed and closed the distance between them.

"Shut up! Did he have you flat on your back or bent over his desk? I want to make sure I get the details right so my nightmares can be as realistic as fucking possible! Tell me, Delia, how much does a young girl's innocence go for these days?" Beatrice demanded.

"I have no idea what you're talking about. How many celebratory drinks did you have—"

But Beatrice slapped her soundly across the face before Cordelia could finish her denial. "I want an answer, Cordelia Anne Wainwright!"

"Mother!" Cordelia had never been hit by anyone in her entire life, let alone by her own mother.

When Cordelia attempted to turn her back on Beatrice, she heard her mother gasp loudly. There on her right shoulder blade was the beginnings of a man's hand-size bruise.

"I'll kill that bastard! Get dressed; we're going to the police!" Beatrice instructed her daughter, enraged at what she perceived to be an act of violence.

"Are you daft, Mother? What am I to tell them? That I willingly let *that man* bend me over his desk, lift up my skirt, put his cock inside of me, and when I squirmed a bit from the...*discomfort*...of it, he held me still by the shoulder for less than two minutes?" Her voice was hollow and flat but quite matter-of-fact. "The price was a three-film contract and £750,000. I leave for Los Angeles for three months the day after tomorrow."

Beatrice was stunned. *How could I have failed you as a mother this much?*

"Was it worth it, Darling? I mean, I hope you enjoyed it at least, considering what it cost you."

"No, Mother, I didn't enjoy it. As a matter of fact, I was sick all over the inside of the taxi on the way home and had to give the driver an extra tenner for his trouble," Cordelia explained, with tears burning down her cheeks. "When I got home, I would've drunk the entire bottle of Listerine if I didn't know it would probably kill me.

"His beard smelled ghastly. And Polo lingers way longer on your skin than you'd think. But now I know, and I'll *never* have to do it again, so in a strange way, I'm happy about that. I made my choice, Mother, and I know you disagree with it, but I'm certain it was right for me."

Beatrice did not agree, nor did she think her daughter believed she'd made the right decision, either. Every fiber of her being wanted to shake Cordelia until she saw what a terrible mistake she'd made, but seeing her daughter at her lowest, with tears nonetheless, Beatrice could not bring herself to do it. Instead, she tried to look toward the positive.

"Perhaps you would *prefer* it more with a woman."

Part III

Ophelia

CHAPTER NINE

"Two Actresses of Irvine"

Feb. 21, 2017: Los Angeles, CA

"Your mother must be very proud of you, then, because you've had great success as an actress. You've spent the last eighteen years churning out great films, but do you regret not starting a family?" Patti intrusively asked.

This fucking bitch!

"I do not see how that is any of your—or anyone else's, for that matter—business, Patti. I am an actress, not some reality star or social media influencer. I make films, not Twitter trends/headlines, or whatever they are called."

* * *

2010-2015: Los Angeles & Irvine, CA

The seven-year itch is an unproven theory regarding marriages that disintegrate into divorce around their seven-year expiration date. Increased arguments, a lack of sexual or emotional intimacy, spending an increased amount of time apart, taking one another for granted, and keeping secrets are the warning signs that your relationship may be on the verge of collapse.

While Cordelia and Aubrey were not legally 'married,' they were in year seven of a committed, dysfunctional, and absolutely absurd relationship.

First, Cordelia was in year twelve of a marriage to a closeted action star, with whom she and Aubrey still cohabitated whenever he was in Los Angeles. It was the most bizarre ménage à trois imaginable, namely because instead of having sex with Bradley, the two women separately used him as their own personal 'marriage' counselor.

Second, only their immediate families, *Frick and Frack*, and a few very trusted gay friends knew they lived with one another. Thanks to Cordelia's third-year anniversary gift, Aubrey now owned the house next to theirs.

Attached to the deed was a handwritten note, etched in black ink: '*It is more frugal to own than rent, Sweetheart.*'

Third, to explain their yearly trips together to St. Albans every Christmastime and summer, Cordelia gave Aubrey half of her ownership in Willowbrook Productions as a third-year Christmas gift. Now, instead of the company making two films per year, it made three—each actress got her own movie in the spring, and they made one together in the fall.

Attached to the contract was a handwritten note, etched in black ink: '*A contract is more binding than a ring, Sweetheart.*'

Fourth, to keep up appearances, Aubrey 'dated' other women. These women, usually young, attractive actresses, lived rent-free in the house next to theirs and got roles in Willowbrook films.

This is how they managed to keep the whispers, well, whispers. Sure, people thought it was odd that two completely opposite personalities and actresses got on so well together.

Cordelia was cold and aloof, and she made emotionally complex films with depressing endings. Aubrey was warm and welcoming, and she made romantically simple films with happy endings. The four films they made together, once Aubrey became a partner at Willowbrook, were all dramas in which they played either friends, sisters, and/or rivals—never lovers.

Cordelia was considered the serious actress who garnered Oscar nominations—her tally was now at five. Aubrey was viewed as the actress who made feel-good films that people went to see on date night. This, along with making films for their own production company as business partners, allowed them to avoid the pitfalls of professional rivalry. That was until both women were nominated for the Best Actress Oscar in the same year— 2015, the seventh year of their romantic partnership.

* * *

Feb. 14-15, 2015: Irvine, CA

Thirty-eight days were between the announced Oscar nominations and the gold statues being handed out to the winners. To Aubrey, those thirty-eight days felt like a year.

There were interviews to give and photos to be taken, and there were so many 'goddamn parties' to attend. Cordelia despised all of these things—especially the 'goddamn parties.' Aubrey immensely enjoyed all of these activities. Still, Cordelia's constant complaining about having to participate in them dampened the overall spirit of what Aubrey had accomplished to be invited to, well, the party. Aubrey chalked up Cordelia's indifference to the 'dog & pony show' to the fact that she'd now been invited to it six times. This, however, was Aubrey's first invite, and she wanted to enjoy it fully.

"Why aren't you dressed yet?" Aubrey asked exasperatedly when she found Cordelia lying in their bed with earbuds in her ears.

"You look nice, Sweetheart. That dress hugs your ass in all the right places," Cordelia said appreciatively when she looked up at Aubrey wearing an off-the-shoulder, body-conforming short-sleeve red Gucci dress.

"It's nine o'clock, Cordy! When I called you from Burbank, you *promised* you'd be ready when I got home!"

"Yes, but then I started listening to this podcast about infectious diseases, and I must have lost track of time," Cordelia explained sheepishly. "Since it is so late already, Sweetheart, perhaps you should go without me… Or, you could let me—"

Aubrey angrily cut her off before she could suggest that she unzip her dress. "Goddamnit, Cordy! If you didn't want to go, you should've just fucking said it—instead of having me drive all the way back here for you to pretend that you ever intended to go in the first place! And then to use the promise of sex to get me to stay—when we haven't made love since Christmas—that's low even for you."

"You should really check that log of our sex life that you keep, *My Love*, because, as I recall, we had sex on your birthday," Cordelia unwisely corrected her.

"Um, that wasn't sex, *mi amor*. That was a lackluster, obligatory attempt on your part to go down on me, which *definitely* didn't satisfy me—I *faked* it, so you could feel that you'd done your duty and I could go to sleep!" Aubrey said hurtfully. Then she turned to leave and yelled, "I'll be home *late*," as she slammed the bedroom door behind her.

And, she most assuredly returned home late, well after 3:00 a.m. She was drunk on 1800 and horny, so she didn't appreciate it when she got into bed naked to find Cordelia's version of a beaver dam: a stack of pillows dividing their respective sides of the bed.

"I *know* you're awake, you pouting child," Aubrey said as she stared at the bedroom ceiling and patted the pillows dividing them in a familiar rhythmic beat: *one pat, double pat, hard smack, and repeat.*

This was not the first pillow fort she'd come home to in their seven years together—and it was at least the tenth one in the past six months.

Silence.

"Goddamnit, Cordy, I swear if you don't turn over and remove those stupid fucking pillows, I'm going to pull out my vibrator, and you can listen to what an actual orgasm sounds like," Aubrey threatened.

Cordelia didn't turn over but dryly said, "Do what you must, Sweetheart, but do make it quick, please. Mother will be calling at seven."

"For fuck's sake, it's Valentine's Day! Isn't that one of your holy days of obligation?" Aubrey sarcastically asked.

"No, *My Love*, it is now February 15th. You missed your opportunity to be unsatisfied by my duty. But there is always St. Patrick's Day to look forward to—perhaps you will get lucky then. Good night."

One pat, double pat, extra hard smack, and repeat.

Aubrey almost pulled out her vibrator, but not out of spite. No, she thought about doing it to see if anything could arouse Cordelia because she had tried everything she could think of or read about on the Internet to reignite her lover's interest in sex— and, more importantly, her.

While Aubrey didn't keep an actual log of their sex life as Cordelia suggested, she knew that if she did, there would be minimal entries over the past six months. They'd had sex, *if that's what you wanted to call it*, exactly four times: their anniversary, Christmas, New Year's Eve, and Aubrey's birthday. This is what she thought about as she lay naked next to the woman she loved and stared at the ceiling in disbelief and frustration.

At thirty and thirty-four years of age, they were far from being an old 'married' couple. Still, Cordelia had reduced any form of intimacy between them to asterisk notations of significant dates in her Letts' planner. And, three of those four *Red 'S' Days*, as Aubrey referred to them, were one-sided and performed as an act of British duty with little enthusiasm. It was only on Christmas night that Cordelia willingly participated in a mutual act of lovemaking. Aubrey suspected that was only because Beatrice forced Cordelia to drink three glasses of wine at dinner to 'loosen her up.'

Their sexual desert began abruptly at the tail-end of their summer holiday in St. Albans without explanation. At first, Aubrey thought it was due to Cordelia's usual homesickness. Yet, then she remembered that this was precisely the time when her lover did her best work in the bedroom—she used sex as a way to recover from her unhappiness at being so far away from her family.

Now, instead of reaching across their bed, Cordelia took extra Prozac and Valium, which only decreased her libido. No matter how hard Aubrey pushed her for an explanation or practically begged her to let her give her what she so *desperately* needed, Cordelia remained silent, slept with her back turned, and her knees locked.

At 6:45 a.m., Aubrey was awakened by a hand on her bare shoulder. A fully-dressed Cordelia stood holding an oversized pajama shirt, a cup of coffee, and three Ibuprofen.

"Here, Sweetheart. Mother will be calling soon." This was her polite British way of saying, *For fuck's sake, make yourself presentable.*

And just like every Sunday when they were in Irvine, the phone rang at 7:00 a.m.

While technology is a beautiful thing, it also has its pitfalls. Namely, instead of speaking to her mother through a receiver, Cordelia was now forced to converse with her over FaceTime.

Beatrice could read her daughter's face like the back of her own hand. For months, she'd known that not only was her daughter miserable but that Aubrey was almost at her breaking point. This is why when they visited at Christmastime, she had done her best to gently shove Cordelia back toward the one person she could trust to care for her fragile daughter—even if it took every bottle in the Wainwright wine cellar.

"You look tired…am I to assume you had a pleasant Valentine's Day, then?" Beatrice hopefully asked.

Aubrey twisted her mouth and pursed her lips. Cordelia weakly smiled and nervously ran a hand through her hair.

"Hmm…so what offensive note and gift did my daughter give to you this year, Dear?" Beatrice joked to lighten what was apparently a dark mood in their bedroom.

"Pillows," Aubrey said through clenched teeth.

"Down, I hope. Yes, I know you think there's a slight possibility of Avian Flu, Delia, but they're much more comfortable than microfiber or latex."

"Yes, Mother."

Beatrice got a distinct feeling that no new pillows were given, but instead, what Aubrey had described to her as 'Cordy's Wall of Isolation.'

"Have you made a wager yet about next week?" Beatrice asked, trying to change the subject. The Oscars were only one week away.

Still fuming from the night before, Aubrey faked a smile. "When I *win*, I think we'll get married."

Without looking at her would-be fiancée, Cordelia laughed. "Do you hear that, Mother? She wishes to have me incarcerated for bigamy over the pillows that I buy."

"Maybe being locked up with a bunch of women would turn you on," Aubrey maliciously sneered.

"Are there mute ones there, then?" Cordelia answered without turning her head.

One pat, double pat, extra hard smack, and repeat was Aubrey's response.

"Have you spoken to Ophy, *yet*?" Beatrice brought up the subject that Cordelia disliked talking about even more than her sex life. *This conversation couldn't possibly get any worse.*

"No, Mother," Cordelia curtly answered. "She texts me when she needs money."

"Remind me, Darling...which one of you is fifteen, and which one of you is closing in on thirty-five?" Beatrice tartly asked.

"Um, I know this! This one builds pillow forts in our bed," Aubrey said pointing at Cordelia.

Cordelia ignored this swipe at her maturity and looked her mother as squarely in the eyes as she could through a screen. "Not only did she go against my wishes, I was *forced* to pay for her wishes with my own goddamn money, Mother."

"For heaven's sake, she's a bloody teenager! What teenager wouldn't rather spend her winter break skiing with her friends than with a house full of middle-aged women? Yes, I know, Darling, you would, but that's because you're...*you*," Beatrice derisively chided her daughter.

"I'm not a middle-aged woman!" Cordelia raised her voice.

"You have the sex drive of one," Aubrey shot back.

Cordelia had had it with the both of them.

First, she turned her ire on Aubrey. "You want fucked at the drop of a hat—start sleeping next door, you fucking nympho!"

Then, it was Beatrice's turn. "I don't pay for a massive house, a goddamn outdated theater, and an outrageously priced boarding school for my family to treat me as an afterthought, a personal ATM, or something to ridicule at their own personal amusement!"

With that, the phone went dead, and she walked out the bedroom without looking back.

* * *

Feb. 22, 2015: Irvine & Los Angeles, CA

Cordelia was already awake when her alarm went off at 6:30 a.m. She sat with her back propped against Aubrey's pillows, staring at the gold-framed reproduction of John Everett Millais' *Ophelia* that hung directly across from her bed.

The painting depicts *Act IV, Scene VII* of *Hamlet*, where Ophelia drowns herself in a brook after her lover, Hamlet, murders her father. Aubrey hated this picture and asked Cordelia to remove it from their bedroom at least once a month. But there it stood, several years after their first night together.

It was depressing to Aubrey, but it was a symbolic reminder to Cordelia of how she ended up looking at a reproduction in Irvine and not the original at the Tate in London. She'd literally sold herself to play the role of Ophelia in Grant Andrews' film adaptation of *Hamlet*.

In Victorian times, actresses were often looked down upon as one step above whores and shunned by polite society. In the year 2000, actresses were given Best Supporting Actress Oscars and lauded by film critics.

'I must, like a whore, unpack my heart with words.'

Instead of drowning in a brook filled with flowers and willows just once, as Ophelia did in *Hamlet*, Cordelia drowned herself every day with guilt and lies. First, she'd sacrificed her girlhood virtue; then came the falsehoods and the regrets that streamed through her mind every day of her life after that.

Had Grant's *Hamlet* been a flop, Cordelia might have been saved from herself. Yet, it was a financial and critical success that made her a star, which inevitably landed her sitting alone in a bed over 8,000 kilometers away from home.

When the phone rang at seven o'clock, she thought about not answering it. She'd not spoken to either Beatrice or Aubrey since the previous Sunday. When she'd returned home later that afternoon, Aubrey had removed both half of her wardrobe and herself to the house next door. She didn't leave a note but, instead, stacked every pillow she could find in the house on her side of their bed.

"Good morning, Mother," Cordelia answered in a false-sounding cheery voice, with an even faker smile plastered on her face.

Beatrice pulled her iPad just a bit closer to see her daughter's icy-blue eyes looking back at her. Her pupils were more dilated than usual.

"Hmm…are we starting off our day with two or three happy pills?"

Silence.

"Where is your *much* better other half?" Beatrice asked, although she already knew the answer. In a normal week, Aubrey called her at least twice; this week, which was far, far, far from normal, she'd called four times.

"Now, come Mother, we both *know* you have spoken with her—but, if I had to venture a guess, she has probably got her legs wrapped around Whitney's face," Cordelia said maliciously.

"Goddamnit, Delia!" Beatrice snapped. "You know very well that isn't true…*yet*. But, if you continue being…*you*, it's only a matter of time before you push her not only out of your bed but out of your life, too—forever."

Silence.

Beatrice rubbed her forehead deeply with the palm of her hand. It was her way of calming herself down when Cordelia was completely out of control. In a more soothing voice, she began again. "Darling, today is a significant day for the both of you. Don't you want to spend it with the woman you love instead of pouting and sneaking looks out of blinds?"

"Did she say I'm doing that? I can assure you there's no remake of *Rear Window* being shot inside this bloody house!" Cordelia said heatedly.

"No, of course not, Darling. But she did say she hadn't heard from or seen you all week. It's not like you to miss work for an entire week. You're lucky Mrs. Holt could confirm you'd eaten every steak and kidney pie in the house; otherwise, we'd have rung for a wellness check. I do hope you'll still fit into your dress after—"

"I'm not going," Cordelia curtly interrupted her.

This was one of those rare moments Beatrice wished she were in *that cesspool of a city* so that she could shake the living hell out of her daughter. Yet, all she could do was attempt to remain calm and keep an even tone.

"*That* would be an *extremely* poor decision on your part, Cordelia Anne Wainwright. Yes, I know you are convinced you shall never win another Oscar because you are 'cursed,' but what happens if *she* wins and you aren't there to congratulate her? Haven't you missed enough life-defining moments with Ophy to learn your lesson *yet*?"

Cordelia sharply countered her mother's low blow. "Drinking venom instead of afternoon tea, are we?"

"Don't blame me for telling you the truth—God knows you avoid it at every turn! This whole idiotic melodrama is *your* fault and no one else's.

"The entire reason for this steep decline in your already outrageous melancholy is that you got your feelings hurt. When Ophy said she no longer wished to call you 'Dilly' because it made her sound like a child, you should've told her right then and there, what she should call you instead!" Beatrice's blood felt as though it were boiling.

"You know very well that I cannot do that!" Cordelia yelled.

"Goddamnit, Delia! How many times have we had this bloody conversation? It's not a matter of 'cannot' but *won't*."

"You *won't* answer for your own decisions and lies. You *won't* tell that poor child that her mother left her as an infant. You *won't* admit that you continue this farce because you don't want to tell her why. And, finally, you *won't* confess to the woman that you sleep beside every night that you are so guilt-ridden by all of your decisions that the only desire you feel is to walk into the ocean and drown yourself! If you *won't* be honest with your daughter, at least tell Aubrey the truth so she can understand and help you with your self-inflicted misery, Darling," Beatrice passionately implored her daughter.

Silence.

Beatrice wearily shook her head in defeat. Then, she put on her strict motherly voice. "As you wish. *But* you are going to that over-hyped awards show to support your partner, who loves and supports you without prejudice—and, God knows, there's *so much* she could find fault with. If you don't, I *will* tell her why. Do you understand me, Cordelia Anne Wainwright?"

"Yes, Mother," Cordelia answered dejectedly, staring at the painting on the wall facing her.

* * *

And, so she went.

Her black Stella McCartney sleeveless gown was a tad snug in the waist, but Spanx helped with that. Bradley helped with her nerves and wobbly legs. He and his Versace tux were her shields on the red carpet, and he answered most of the inane questions thrown her way. Her mother, of course, was right—she'd once again begun overmedicating, and she had raided Bradley's hidden bookcase stash of its vodka, too.

When they were finally seated next to Aubrey and her 'date,' Whitney Simon, in the Dolby Theatre, Cordelia said little and put on her camera-ready smile. Aubrey knew immediately by the extraordinarily glassy look in her lover's blue eyes and her less-than-perfect posture that she was *high as a fucking kite.*

Aubrey flagged down an usher and requested he bring them as many bottles of water as he could carry. Once he returned, Aubrey took off the lid and handed a bottle to Cordelia, "Start drinking!" She said it with a smile, but her voice was razor-sharp.

Cordelia's speech was slurred when she loudly protested, "I'm already bloated enough in this goddamn dress."

Still smiling but raging inside, Aubrey leaned over and whispered into her ear, "I'm going to speak, and you're going to listen, got it? Nod your head if you understand."

Cordelia lazily nodded.

"You *will* drink every fucking ounce of water that I give you. When you're ready to go to the bathroom, I *will* take you. When I win, you *will* smile and not pull away when I hug and kiss you on the cheek. Then, when we go home tonight, I *will* confiscate those fucking pills and hand them out to you like the child that you are. Do you understand me, *mi amor?*"

Instead of nodding, Cordelia began drinking.

* * *

When they got home after a deathly silent ride in the back of a limo—they'd left Bradley and Whitney to attend the Vanity Fair after-party without them—Aubrey went straight to their bedroom and placed her Best Actress Oscar right next to Cordelia's Best Supporting Actress one on the bookshelf. Then she struggled with the zipper of her red strapless Chanel gown, unceremoniously threw it on the walk-in closet floor, and violently jerked one of her oversized shirts off its hanger and struggled to button it up—her hands were shaking with rage.

As she washed her makeup off in the bathroom sink, she heard Cordelia finally make her way into their bedroom.

"Turn around, so I can unzip you," Aubrey said matter-of-factly as she patted her face dry with a towel.

Cordelia did as she was told. When she was undressed, Aubrey ushered her into the shower, and then tore their room apart looking for pill bottles. She found five, which she angrily threw into her nightstand drawer.

Then, she got into bed and waited. And, there it was, staring straight at her furiously burning light-brown eyes—that *hideous, depressing* picture. She'd finally had enough of its mocking, so she got out of bed and practically ripped it off the wall, carried it down the hallway, and threw it out the front door, which caused the glass to shatter everywhere.

When she returned to the bedroom, she could hear Cordelia was finally out of the shower and brushing her teeth. Aubrey whipped the bathroom door open like a tornado.

"You ruined what was supposed to be one of the biggest nights of my life. What were you thinking, you fucking child? Haven't I supported you and your countless *afflictions*? Don't I go along with your ridiculous demands that we keep our relationship a secret— it's fucking 2015, Cordy! No one cares anymore if we fuck, or, in our case, don't fuck!

"I swear to God, if you *ever* do something like this again, I will call a press conference and tell anyone who will listen how I have been in an emotionally abusive, sexually frustrating relationship with you since you were my fucking boss. Do you understand me?" Aubrey was seething.

Cordelia was flossing her teeth during the entire tirade. When she was done, she took a big swig from her Listerine cap and rinsed her mouth. Then, she asked, "So, to be clear, you would *prefer* that we not fuck tonight, Sweetheart?"

Her answer was a death glare as Aubrey turned sharply away and got into bed and built her own pillow fort.

One pat, double pat, extra, extra hard smack, and repeat.

CHAPTER TEN

"A Summer Night's Wedding"

March-May 2015: Irvine, CA

They spent the following three months after the Oscars both together and separately. Each was working on their own individual film and drove together every weekday morning to the studio in silence. Before they exited Aubrey's 2015 red Lexus RC350 Coupe at approximately 7:00 a.m., Cordelia was dispensed one 60mg Prozac for the day and they went their separate ways.

They didn't eat lunch together, and whenever they had production company meetings with Geoffrey he would do most of the talking. At Aubrey's insistence, shooting always wrapped by 7:00 p.m. Then she drove them back home, and they ate whatever English food Mrs. Holt had prepared—again, in abject silence.

Ten o'clock was bedtime. There was no need for the pillow fort anymore because neither woman would dare attempt to reach across the bed for the other. Cordelia refused to apologize, and Aubrey refused to give in and forgive her without one. Obviously, there was no sex, but there also weren't any half-hearted goodnight kisses on the cheek or a single 'I love you,' either. They slept with their backs turned to the other—Waiting.

On the weekends, Aubrey left the house after a silent breakfast of English toffee scones or poached eggs and toast and didn't return until well after 9:00 p.m.—and sometimes, based on whom she was with, after midnight. While she was gone to 'who the fuck knows where,' Cordelia either slept or listened to her podcasts in bed. It didn't matter how drunk Aubrey got on 1800 anymore; she never slid her legs up Cordelia's or ran her fingers down her *mi amor*'s spine.

Their 7:00 a.m. Sunday chats with Beatrice were the only time they actively engaged with one another. They recounted what had transpired on their respective sets, and Beatrice gave her own accounting of the spring shows at the Wainwright and what needed to be fixed or replaced at the house and/or the theater. There was no mention of Ophy or their lack of communication and intimacy with one another. Of course, this was unnecessary because Beatrice heard it all during her bi-weekly calls with Aubrey.

"I could feel her staring at my back for hours...Why won't she say she's sorry? I'm not sure how much longer I can stay..."

All Beatrice could say was that things would be different when they came to St. Albans. Aubrey wasn't hopeful.

* * *

June 15-17, 2015: St. Albans, England

The house in St. Albans now had two small children running about it, courtesy of Miranda and Clark. Olivia, age four, and Desi, age two, were constant reminders of how little connected Cordelia and Aubrey were. For obvious reasons, they couldn't have children together, but when Aubrey had suggested in Year Five that one of them could do IVF, Cordelia had looked at her as though she'd lost her mind. The subject was never broached again.

Perhaps it was the screaming children or a need to escape her mother's constant scrutiny, but Portia now lived in London with her boyfriend, Roy. As the youngest sister, she was relegated to playing lesser roles at the Wainwright. This suited her fine because it gave her less responsibility and more time to party with Roy and his posh friends. Beatrice found her lifestyle frivolous and told her so at every opportunity.

"Thirty-year-old women should focus on their careers and/or their families rather than where the next party is."

And then there were Aubrey and Cordelia. They had careers, no marriage, no children, and the only party they attended together was a pity party. Aubrey looked at Miranda, Olivia, and Desi with envy, while Cordelia looked upon them with regret.

Her sister was happily married, had two sweet—but *so noisy and messy*—daughters, and a career and life that could have been hers. She despised Miranda, which was conveyed in every syllable she spoke to her.

"Must you let your brats run about as devil spawns? For fuck's sake, why are your children so goddamn messy?"

Miranda, of course, took it in stride—she knew it wasn't really her children that made her older sister a complete and total bitch. Once she became a mother, she understood Cordelia's malice toward her, and as long as nothing was said directly to her girls, she let her sister's snide remarks slide off her back.

Ophy was now to be called Ophelia—like 'Dilly,' 'Ophy' was too childish for a fifteen-year-old girl who didn't need to be picked up at the train station by *Delia* anymore. She'd grown into the spitting image of her mother and aunts—tall, slender, blue-eyed, and with a head of gorgeous strawberry-blond hair. She wore short skirts and shorts, tight tank tops, makeup, and a flirtatious smile.

"Have you spoken to Ophy about what we discussed *yet*?" Beatrice archly asked Cordelia as they played Bridge with Miranda and Aubrey in the living room after dinner.

"Must you disturb our peaceful respite from the demon spawns?" Cordelia irritably asked as she rearranged the cards in her hands—Clark had *thankfully* carried the children off to bed.

"Would you like to have another one running about soon?" Beatrice pointedly looked across the table at her eldest daughter.

"She doesn't even really have a boyfriend, Mother. So, I see no need to put her on birth control."

This drew Aubrey's attention away from her own cards. "Cordy's the last person who should be discussing sex and birth control with her."

These conversations were a lot easier when Beatrice just prayed for Aubrey. Now, they were like walking through a minefield.

"Delia, to the best of my knowledge, is the only one here familiar with...both sides of the bed. Ophy's generation is just so sexually fluid that it would be best if we cover all avenues. Heaven knows she's also the best person to explain the dangers of STDs. And, besides, no teenager wants to hear about sex from a fifty-six-year-old woman," Beatrice reasoned.

"Um, but she wants to learn about it from a thirty-five-year-old child who didn't have an actual orgasm that wasn't self-induced until she was twenty-eight—and who hasn't had one in six months?" Aubrey was incredulous.

The Wainwrights looked at one another for possible answers to very reasonable questions.

"Sweetheart—" Cordelia began.

"Don't you fucking call me 'Sweetheart' now!" Aubrey quickly cut her off. "You've had almost four months to do it, along with apologizing for your reprehensible behavior or reaching across our fucking bed instead of pouting and staring at my back all fucking night. That is exactly why you're the *last* person who should be discussing anything to do with sex or intimacy with a teenage girl who is more mature than you are!"

"Perhaps she is right, Mother—" Cordelia attempted to reason with Beatrice.

"Nonsense!" It was said vehemently and in a way that dared to be challenged. "You *will* do it, Cordelia Anne Wainwright! Do you understand me?"

"Yes, Mother," Cordelia almost whispered, averting the look of bewilderment in Aubrey's light-brown eyes and yet again rearranging the cards in her hands.

* * *

When they went to bed later that same evening, it was Cordelia who felt Aubrey's eyes boring down on her back. As usual, little was said between them when they changed into their sleeping clothes, and Cordelia performed her various hygienic routines. No kisses or terms of endearment were exchanged when she took her side of the bed and turned her back to Aubrey—but there was a look in Aubrey's eyes that she had never seen before that unnerved her. It was profoundly plain that Aubrey wanted to hear or say something—Cordelia was unsure of which.

After waiting thirty minutes for whatever she wanted, Aubrey softly said, "Cordy, please, turn over."

Silence.

"Cordy, we've slept in the same bed for nearly seven years. Do you think I don't know when you're really asleep? If you love me, you will turn over this minute—don't make me beg you, *mi amor.*" She sounded so, well, *desperate.*

Cordelia slowly turned and rolled over onto her other side to face Aubrey. They lay there silently looking at each other for what seemed like ages, imploring the other to say something—*Anything.*

For Cordelia, there were only two options. She could confess to the woman that she loved that her youngest 'sister' was her daughter and that she'd been lying to her for seven years. Or, she could admit she was sorry and mean it on many levels.

"*My Love*, I've treated you abominably, and I'm truly sorry. I'll try much harder to be worthy of your love and patience. I promise." And she meant it.

She understood Cordelia wasn't telling her the whole truth—she, like Beatrice, knew that the woman she loved more than anything in the entire world only used contractions when she was nervous or evading scrutiny. But Aubrey didn't care, at least that's what she told herself, because she ached to be held, kissed, and caressed.

"Prove it, *mi amor*." She reached across the divide that had separated them for so long and pulled Cordelia toward her. She took both her hands and cupped Cordelia's face and looked her lover directly in her icy-blue eyes before kissing her and whispered in her raspy voice, "I *know* what you refuse to confess to me, *mi amor*, but I still *love* you no matter what. Do you understand?"

Cordelia nodded, and that was all that was needed.

* * *

When Aubrey stretched her arm across the bed the following morning, she wasn't shocked to find it empty—it was Cordelia's signature calling card. She didn't care because what had transpired between them the night before was like nothing she'd experienced in all their years together. Cordelia had given herself completely to Aubrey and wept like a newborn child in Aubrey's arms— Aubrey had never seen Cordelia cry except on film. No words were spoken, but they now fully understood one another.

In the recesses of her mind, Aubrey had always known that Cordelia's reluctance to fully commit to their relationship wasn't a matter of other people discovering that she was a lesbian. Cordelia could care less what outsiders thought about her—her personality made that quite apparent.

What Cordelia truly valued were the opinions of her loved ones. That is why she had such a difficult relationship with her mother, who knew all of her darkest secrets. It is also why she refused to admit that she loved Aubrey for so long—because Aubrey didn't know those same dark secrets.

When she honestly considered Cordelia's adamant insistence that they spend every Christmas and summer in St. Albans, it all made perfect sense—these were the times that Ophy was also at home. The almost crippling homesickness she endured when they returned to America was a direct result of this.

Then, there were the weekly Sunday morning calls to St. Mary's—Cordelia never called Portia or Miranda. And, it was Cordelia, not Beatrice, who paid for everything the child needed or wanted and made all of the decisions regarding Ophy's upbringing.

Finally, Aubrey could rationalize why their last year together had been so fraught with unhappiness and why Cordelia had turned inside herself and away from her.

First, Ophy had unknowingly taken away Cordelia's only acknowledged link to their bond to one another by announcing that she would no longer call her 'Dilly' but 'Delia,' as both Miranda and Portia did. Second, she had decided that she would rather spend most of her winter break with her friends and not in St. Albans, even when Cordelia explained that they already saw one another too little.

Ophy's ungrateful teenage response was, "Isn't it enough that I have to spend the entire summer in St. Albans, Delia?"

Yes, she had questions as to how Ophy came to be in the first place—Cordelia's sexual inexperience when they first became lovers was more than apparent. Why did the entire Wainwright family, except Ophy, pretend she was Beatrice's daughter? And, what could ever possess Cordelia to carry on with such a farce when anyone who knew the truth could see that it brought her such abject misery? But these were questions that Aubrey knew she couldn't ask. It was enough, for now, that she knew the most important truth.

A weaker woman would have been livid that she'd been misled. She couldn't say outright lied to because Cordelia, nor any of the adult Wainwright women, had ever referred to Ophy as her sister in all the years they'd been together—she was just Ophy.

Had Aubrey put the puzzle pieces together when she was twenty-five and less secure about what she meant to Cordelia, she probably would've packed her bags and never looked back. But at thirty, with nearly seven years of dealing with and accepting all Cordelia's peculiarities, Aubrey was willing to overlook this glaring omission because she loved her unconditionally—and if their last year of hell together didn't push her out the door, nothing could.

As it was past 9:00 a.m. on a Thursday, she knew perfectly well that Cordelia was gone to the Wainwright and would not return until dinner. So, she got up to shower, but as she was going to the bathroom, she noticed an envelope addressed to her sitting atop the black, gold-inlaid desk.

Inside was a handwritten note, etched in black ink: *'You will find in the center drawer of this desk what you are owed, My Love & My Wife.'*

As Aubrey slowly slid the always locked drawer open, she saw resting in the center of Ophy's birth certificate a Van Cleef & Arpels platinum solitaire diamond wedding ring.

* * *

When Beatrice saw Aubrey practically float into the dining room at 6:30 p.m., she instantly knew that her daughter had *finally* done something right. She had no idea what that could be, but she was sure it wasn't the result of a *good and proper bedding*—she'd seen that particular look many times before. This was very different.

"Where have you been all day, Dear? Did you go to town to buy a new dress?" Beatrice asked as she scanned Aubrey's short, form-fitting white sleeveless dress.

Your firm bottom and never-ending shapely legs are definitely what attracted Delia to you.

Aubrey giggled like a schoolgirl. "Do you think Cordy will like it? She *prefers* me in red."

"The family will count their blessings if she doesn't ravish you right here at the table before dessert is served," Beatrice joked. "Good heavens, I have never seen you look so beautiful and, dare I say it, happy. Tell me, Dear, is she really that good in bed? Is that why you've stayed with her all these years when anyone else would have dropped her long ago? I'd think there are certain... *acts*...that she'd be unwilling to perform."

A wicked laugh escaped from Aubrey, who knew Cordelia would be outraged by this conversation. "I stay with her because I love her and couldn't imagine my life without her in it.

"But...yes...when she fully commits to it, she is the best lover I've ever had—and she enjoys having one particular *act* performed on her too much not to reciprocate. No one takes direction better than Cordelia Wainwright."

At that, they both cackled like two witches flying under a full moon.

"What is so funny, then?" Cordelia asked as she, Clark, and Miranda joined them in the dining room.

The witches said nothing but looked at one another knowingly and smiled.

When Cordelia sat down beside Aubrey, she did her best not to stare at Aubrey's bare legs and naked left hand. "You look very…" Cordelia stammered.

"Hot!" Portia finished her oldest sister's unfinished thought as she and Ophy entered the room. "Hello, Mother. I thought I'd come for dinner if that's all right."

"Of course, Darling. Eating instead of drinking your dinner once a week is highly recommended," Beatrice quipped.

This was the first time Beatrice's family, sans the babies, had all been seated around the dining table since the previous summer, and she was ecstatic. She would have thought it was the perfect night if it weren't for the mischievous smiles that continuously passed between Aubrey, Portia, Miranda, and Ophy throughout dinner. Cordelia, as usual, was completely oblivious and seemed preoccupied with Aubrey's legs and left hand.

When dessert was served, the picture became much clearer. Mrs. Holt had been dispatched from her grandchildren to bake a simple two-tier white wedding cake with pink decorative roses.

"Mrs. Holt, what on Earth are you doing here?" Cordelia confusedly asked as her cook wheeled out the cake.

"Ms. Aubrey invited me to your wedding, Ms. Delia. This is my wedding gift to you."

"But…" Cordelia stammered.

"Yes, *mi amor*, we all know that you're already legally married," Aubrey said as she stood. "But I want us to be *really* married. That means pledging ourselves to one another in front of our family—not leaving notes saying: 'I lost a wager, here's a ring, and now you're my wife, the end.'"

"Delia!" Beatrice was outraged.

"Mother, that's…" Cordelia fruitlessly tried to explain.

"Stand up!" Aubrey demanded and held out her hand, which held two rings—the one Cordelia had left for her in the drawer and a simple platinum wedding band Aubrey had bought in town that afternoon.

"I already have one of those, thank you," Cordelia said as she uneasily stood.

"That one can *rent* space on your right hand when we're in LA. But this," Aubrey said as she grabbed Cordelia's left hand with her right one, "is now *owned* by me—and every inch of you, from now on. In God's eyes, this *ring* is more *binding* than any legal contract, Cordelia Anne Wainwright; it is freely given without reservation as a symbol of my love and devotion to you, *forever*."

And, before Cordelia knew it, she stared in disbelief at a *new* ring on her left hand.

"Darling, surely you've played this scene at least once in one of your depressing films and know that it's now your turn to say your lines," Beatrice gibed as she stood and took the ring that had belonged to her own mother, which she'd given to Cordelia *five* years ago for this very moment, from the palm of Aubrey's hand and gave it to her mute daughter. "For heaven's sake, Delia, take her hand and tell her how you feel about her."

So, Cordelia took Aubrey's left hand and said the first thing that sprung to her mind. "I'm going to speak, and you're going to listen, got it? Nod your head if you understand."

Aubrey did as she was told, but her eyes were filled with tears, and not shock, as Cordelia's had been the first time she'd said those exact words to her.

"I love you, Aubrey May Taylor, and I am so happy each time you say it back to me, be it raspy whispers in my ear or in your actions. Every time you goofily smile at me, I know you love me. Every time your soft, pouty lips kiss mine, I know that you love me. Every time you reach across our bed and rub those sexy legs up mine and seductively run your fingertips down my spine, I know you love me. And I know you love me because you stay with me no matter what. I give this ring freely and without reservation to my beautiful, patient wife as a symbol of my love and devotion to you, *forever.*"

The family rarely saw public displays of affection between the now-married couple. Yet, once that platinum solitaire diamond wedding ring was secured on her left hand, Aubrey used that same hand to pull Cordelia's head down toward hers and kissed her with such passion that any questions about what went on between them in the bedroom were explicitly answered.

"Right...we shall have cake before consummation!" Beatrice declared, blushing.

* * *

Aubrey didn't need to reach across the bed the next morning when she woke up at well past nine because Cordelia was tightly pressed against her back. Evidently, marriage was the one thing that could keep her from going to work.

"Are you playing hooky, *Mrs.* Wainwright?" Aubrey purred as she felt Cordelia's hand glide up the length of the inside of her thigh.

"Definitely," Cordelia wantonly whispered into the nape of Aubrey's neck. "Afterward..." she breathlessly said as she fully nudged Aubrey's legs apart with her knee, "I thought *we* might talk to Ophy about the birds and bees."

"You don't need my help explaining that subject to her—" Aubrey grunted as she felt Cordelia's strap-on roughly slide inside of her.

"But I need you, Sweetheart..." Cordelia breathlessly pleaded.

"Obviously...not so fucking fast, Cordy," Aubrey said bossily.

Her new wife had two personalities when it came to sex, depending on the time of day. At night, she was slow and attentive Cordy, and they made love, but on a rare morning that she slept in, she was fast and aggressive Ms. Wainwright, and they fucked. Aubrey much *preferred* Cordy because Ms. Wainwright wanted to get off as quickly as possible so she could go to work.

"If you are much gentler and promise to stop talking about your daughter when we're *making love*, I'll do whatever you want," Aubrey bargained.

Cordelia slowed her pace and somewhat jokingly asked, "Will you use coasters and not throw wet towels on the floor?"

"Yes…and I'll even stop using your toothbrush when you piss me off."

Aubrey laughed—Cordelia not so much.

* * *

Once they were freshly showered and Cordelia replaced her old toothbrush with a new one, they found Ophy in her room watching YouTube videos on her phone.

Certain conversations between parents and their children are so very uncomfortable. First, as a parent, you can't really imagine that one day your daughter is going to be giving a blow-job in the front seat of a car or that she'd willingly allow someone to penetrate her from behind and let her ass be slapped while it was done. Second, teenagers already know so much more about sex than you think they do that you are the one who ends up embarrassed by your own ignorance.

Cordelia was not this parent—she listened to way too many podcasts for that. Still, Cordelia looked as though she might be sick when she said to Aubrey, "*My Love*, please don't judge me for what's about to happen."

Having worked with Cordelia on six films, Aubrey was familiar with how her wife transformed herself into a character: blue eyes closed, two deep breaths, and three head shakes to the side.

This happened right before Cordelia matter-of-factly asked, "Right, what do you know about sex, Ophelia?"

"Which kind?" Ophy wisecracked.

Cordelia's face was already on fire. "Any kind that you may have *already* engaged in?"

Aubrey couldn't believe her ears. Cordelia loved having sex but abhorred talking about it.

"Well, I like blokes, so you might not know much about that—"

Cordelia immediately cut off her daughter's snideness, "I'm not as completely ignorant on the subject as you might think.

Contrary to what you may believe, Aubrey wasn't the first person to penetrate me. Are you still a virgin, then?"

"Cordy!" Aubrey exclaimed in shock at her wife's boldness.

Cordelia ignored her and carried on full steam. "Well, let's have it then. Fingers in your pants, cock in your mouth or inside of you—either orifice, please be specific—I need to know which one so when I take you to the gynecologist, I can tell her what tests to run. Untreated syphilis, gonorrhea, genital warts, and chlamydia are very serious STDs."

Both Ophy and Aubrey just stared at her in unmitigated disbelief. Aubrey had never heard her speak so vividly about sex. She'd once asked Cordelia to talk dirty to her in bed and been told, "I am not a prostitute, Sweetheart."

Although her face was burning red, Cordelia would not be denied her answer. "I asked you a question, Ophelia Anne Wainwright!"

"I've only been kissed and...once, I let Robby touch my boobs," Ophy embarrassedly answered.

Cordelia smiled, leaned forward, and patted her on the head. "Good girl. On Monday, we'll take you to the gynecologist and get you sorted out with birth control—for when you're ready for those sorts of activities and, besides, it'll help regulate your periods. We might ask for a prescription for cramps, you can get quite bitchy sometimes. But you should still make the bloke wear a condom—we've watched enough programs that you know the risks associated with unprotected shagging. We'll get STD pamphlets from the gynecologist so that you can study, and then I'll quiz you...

"And, if you like, afterward, we can go to one of those...sex shops, and you can pick out a...vibrator—I assume you *now* know what that's used for. My mother gave me pornographic videos to watch with mine; they were quite instructional about how to pleasure myself, so you may have some of those, too. Right, well, good chat, then," she awkwardly smiled and walked out of the room without another word.

As uncomfortable smiles passed between Aubrey and Ophy, the girl hesitantly asked, "Does she speak like *that* to you in..."

Aubrey chuckled, "In bed? Only on accident." Aubrey could see how traumatized Ophy was by her introduction to Ms. Wainwright and saw an opportunity. "Um...maybe if you went back to calling her *Dilly* instead of *Delia*, she'd be a bit more... *gentler* when choosing her words with you," Aubrey suggested and smiled as she left the room.

She found Cordelia vigorously brushing her teeth in their bathroom.

"Didn't you just do that?" Aubrey asked as she leaned against the doorframe and grinned.

After she gargled Listerine for thirty seconds, Cordelia finally answered, "I had to wash the filth out of my mouth."

"Um, I thought it was kinda hot—not that you said those things to your daughter, of course—but it did remind me of when Ms. Wainwright used to verbally abuse me because she *desperately* wanted my fingers in her pants but didn't know how to ask. My goodness, how things have changed." Aubrey laughed and put her arms around Cordelia's neck.

"That's because you're a pervert, Sweetheart. I swear, Aubrey, I don't know if I can take her into one of those places—I've actually never been to one," Cordelia sheepishly admitted.

Aubrey bit her lip in order not to laugh. "Um, I sorta knew that, *mi amor*. Let's make a deal. Since you love going to the doctor, you take her to her gyno appointment and teach her about the dangers of STDs, and, if she wants, I'll take her to the sex shop...and if she has any questions I can answer them without traumatizing her anymore."

"I would *prefer* that very much, *My Love*." Cordelia kissed her wife's forehead in gratitude.

"And, I would *prefer* it if that version of Ms. Wainwright visited our bed from time to time—I'll buy her a whole crate of new toothbrushes."

CHAPTER ELEVEN

"The Unmerry Wives of Wainwright"

Sept.—Nov. 2015: Irvine, CA

When the newlyweds returned to the States in September, their relationship was never better. They'd spent the remainder of their summer holiday in St. Albans in complete bliss. They made love every night, and Cordelia often went to town much later than 8:00 a.m. during the week—and sometimes, not at all. The Wainwrights and Aubrey had never experienced this version of Cordelia. Gone were the mood swings, harsh words, and, for the most part, self-loathing.

As Aubrey had suggested, Ophy returned to calling Cordelia 'Dilly,' which only increased her apparent joy. This also allowed Ophy not to be completely mortified by what Aubrey could only imagine would have been a summer holiday filled with explicit sex education tutorials led by Ms. Wainwright herself. Instead, she was kind *Dilly*, who held her daughter's hand when feet went into stirrups, and foreign objects found their way into the pelvic region. There were STD quizzes, of course, but they were handwritten in etched black ink and placed discreetly on Ophy's bed. As for what went on at *that place*, Cordelia didn't want to know, and Aubrey did her best not to laugh at her wife's thunderously loud knocks on Ophy's door whenever she was late for dinner.

Miranda's young daughters were *tolerable*, which improved what had been a fractious sisterly relationship for many years. Now, when Cordelia spoke to her sister, it was as pleasant as she ever got—somewhere between dry wit and total bitch. When the girls wildly ran about the house touching everything with their germ-infested, dirty hands and not using tissues to wipe their runny noses, Cordelia put her earbuds in and made mental notes of where to use Clorox wipes once they *thankfully* disappeared from whichever room she was currently trapped in with them.

But no one was more pleased about the new-and-improved Cordelia Anne Wainwright than Beatrice. While it was never discussed openly, she was confident that Aubrey *finally* knew the truth—*or some version of it*—about Ophy. She understood that her daughter would've never given Aubrey her grandmother's wedding ring otherwise.

When Beatrice had handed Cordelia the ring at the end of the first summer Aubrey had spent with them, it came with a codicil: "This is the woman for you, Darling. Try not to muck it up because I cannot wait another decade for you to be human again. My mother's ring should not be given under false pretenses; do you *understand* me?"

Cordelia agreed, and while Beatrice was most unsatisfied that it took another five years to emerge from the locked middle drawer of the black, gold-inlaid desk, it had *finally* happened when she least expected it. Like Aubrey, she'd thought this might be her daughter-in-law's last summer in St. Albans.

While the now public displays of affection between the two wives were a tad uncomfortable for a household filled with buttoned-up Brits, no one said anything when hello and goodbye kisses lingered indecently too long or when Cordelia's hand scandalously ran up the length of Aubrey's leg when she was ready for bed at nine o'clock every night. They averted their eyes, suppressed their blushes, and thanked God that Cordelia was unequivocally happy.

But St. Albans is St. Albans, and Los Angeles is Los Angeles, which meant that their return to the States found them in a precarious situation.

Cordelia was still married to Bradley in America, and Aubrey was still single. Cordelia's new platinum wedding band was so much like her old one, which now rested on her right hand, that no one would have noticed. However, Aubrey's new piece of bling, which she refused to take off, 'Over my dead fucking body,' drew a lot of unwanted attention.

"Sweetheart, would it not be more prudent to just wear it at home?" Cordelia cautiously asked as Aubrey drove them to the studio on their first day back on set.

The pillow tapping was now replaced with steering wheel pats: *One pat, double pat, hard smack, and repeat.*

"*My Love*, how will you rationally explain a two-carat diamond wedding band mysteriously appearing on your finger after spending three months with me in London?"

"Um, that we're married," Aubrey steadily said without taking her eyes off the road.

"But we're not really married, Sweetheart," Cordelia unwisely said.

Aubrey's head violently snapped toward her wife's seat. "What the fuck did you just say to me?"

Cordelia knew instantly that she'd said the worst thing imaginable. "Legally, of course…You are my wife in all the ways that matter, Sweetheart," Cordelia attempted to say in her most soothing voice.

Aubrey was not soothed but instead incensed. "I'm going to speak, and you're going to listen, got it? Nod your head if you understand."

Oh, dear God, not again. Cordelia nodded.

"I'm not taking this ring off except when I'm being filmed. No woman on Earth has earned her goddamn wedding ring more than me!

"As if your insufferable mood swings; fatty English diet; insane hygiene regimens; addiction to *mood* stabilizers; and overbearing need for order and cleanliness weren't enough, you forgot to tell me—for *seven* fucking years, Cordy—that you have a daughter!

"So, *no*, it would not be 'more prudent' for me to wear it only at home, and I don't give a fuck if people notice it or not. And, if you *ever* say to me again that we aren't *really* married, I'll show you just how married we aren't and leave you and your myriad of *afflictions*. Do you understand me, *mi amor*?"

It was said with such a calm, cold resolve that it could not be misunderstood by anyone—not even Cordelia. Yet, sometimes, she just didn't know when to leave things well enough alone.

"Perhaps, Sweetheart, you could wear it—"

"Don't *fucking* say it!" Aubrey yelled, anticipating her wife's next words: 'on your right hand.'

One pat, double pat, hard smack, and repeat.

And, so, the platinum two-carat solitaire wedding ring remained on Aubrey's left hand. It also stayed in the gossip rags, on *TMZ*, and as a trending topic on Twitter and Instagram for months. To avoid the much *louder* whispers, Cordelia removed Bradley's ring from her right hand, which suited Aubrey fine.

* * *

Christmastime 2015: St. Albans, England

While Beatrice had known for months, what with her bi-weekly calls from her daughter-in-law and her weekly Sunday morning chats with both wives, the rest of the Wainwrights learned at Christmastime that the honeymoon was definitely over for the newlyweds. Gone were the uncomfortable public displays of affection and Cordelia's tolerance for Miranda's 'demon spawns.'

Not even Ophy was immune from Cordelia's mounting frustration with her wife's intransigent stance on how she would wear the 'symbol of their commitment' to one another—which was talked about incessantly by the press and Internet trolls.

When Ophy asked two days before Christmas to go skiing, yet again, with her friends after the holiday, the answer was a resounding, "Unless you're planning on slagging your way across the slopes to pay for it, absolutely fucking not!"

The poor girl was so shocked by Dilly's answer that she burst into tears and hid in her room until Christmas morning.

Beatrice said nothing about her oldest daughter's behavior, which Aubrey found unbelievable. This woman never minced her words when it came to Cordelia. Yet, Beatrice was utterly silent regarding Cordelia's unkind words and brutal belligerence for the first time in all the years that she'd known her mother-in-law. Instead, Beatrice took deep, calming breaths, clenched her jaw, and rubbed her forehead deeply with the palm of her hand.

Not even the rudest gift that Aubrey had ever received from Cordelia—and there had been *many*—elicited a response.

On Christmas morning, Aubrey opened her *gift* to find a first edition, complete set of Tolkien's *The Lord of the Rings*, with an attached handwritten note, etched in black ink: '*Now you have no excuse to not fully comprehend just how dangerous one ring can be, Mrs. Wainwright.*'

As the entire family diverted their eyes from the scene, Aubrey looked toward a mute Beatrice, who wearily shook her head.

After an extremely tense traditional English Christmas dinner, where Cordelia drank four glasses of wine between scowls at Miranda's messy-eating children and having her hand repeatedly slapped from Aubrey's thigh underneath the table, they went to bed.

Per usual, Cordelia took a twenty-minute shower and spent another ten minutes tending to her oral hygiene. When she emerged from the bathroom wearing an open black silk robe and nothing else, she found her wife sitting in bed propped up against her pillows, wearing a festive green Christmas tree pajama set and her glasses, reading her Christmas *gift*.

"Are we playing a sexy librarian scenario tonight, *My Love*?" Cordelia asked in what passed for her lecherous tone.

Aubrey looked up at her wife and studied her almost-naked form intently. "Um, you look like you've put on weight, Cordy.

You should probably cut back on your Christmas puddings… and, maybe the wine, too." Then she went back to reading while simultaneously trying to suppress a smirk.

As a teenage girl, Cordelia could care less about her appearance, but as a woman renowned for her beauty and svelte figure, this dig was like a slap in the face. When she first came to Hollywood, she soon learned that she was what was considered 'elegantly beautiful'—at least, that's what the trades and reviews said. Yet, she never actually viewed herself to be, for lack of a better term, 'hot' until Aubrey explicitly told her how much her rock-hard stomach and firm, full breasts turned her on.

After she hung her robe on the footboard post, she slid into their bed and turned to face Aubrey, who didn't seem to notice that she was waiting for her to put the book down.

"Do you intend to read that bloody book all night?" Cordelia asked irritably.

"Yes, I have three more after I finish this one and there's this strange language—Sindarin…that's difficult to follow. I may need to take notes so I can 'fully comprehend' what is being said," Aubrey said behind a smile.

Did she really mean to call me fat over a stupid note?

Cordelia did her best to shake that unpleasant thought from her head as she edged her body closer to Aubrey's. Then she tried again. "I thought, perhaps, with it being Christmas, we might fully comprehend one another's bodies."

Aubrey burst into laughter. "No wonder you were practically a virgin when I found you—can't you get a screenwriter to write you some better come-on lines?"

"For fuck's sake, Aubrey! First, you call me fat, and now you want to humiliate me for not talking to you like a whore…this is most unkind when all I want to do is have sex with my wife," Cordelia said in her pouty voice.

Aubrey snapped the book shut abruptly but left her glasses on. "What kind of sex do you want to have, *mi amor*?"

Cordelia looked at her confusedly.

Aubrey shook her head exasperatedly. "Do you want to make love with me, or do you want to fuck me? Because if Ms.

Wainwright wants to pin me down to the bed and roughly fuck me like some man until she gets off, the answer is no—my cervix has had enough of that these last few months. But…if Cordy wants to make love with and to her wife, with soft kisses and caresses, *gentle* strokes, and *eye contact*, I might say yes, *if*…you apologize."

There are many, many, many things that Cordelia despised, and apologizing was near the top of the list.

"Right, well, what exactly would I be apologizing for, then?" she asked skeptically.

"If you have to ask, you're obviously not sorry," Aubrey said and reopened her book.

"Are you refusing me, then?"

In all of their years together, Aubrey had never said no to sex. Yes, there had been complaints and demands, but never denials.

"Yes, *mi amor*, I'm *sorry*, but that is exactly what I'm doing," Aubrey answered without turning her attention away from the book.

Cordelia was incensed. "So, to be perfectly fucking clear, in less than five minutes, you've not only insinuated that I'm fat and ridiculed my prior lack of sexual experience, but now you're refusing to have sex with me because I don't know what I'm supposed to be sorry for?"

Again, Aubrey didn't look up from her book. "Your *comprehension* is completely accurate."

With that, Cordelia swiftly rolled over and turned her back to Aubrey, who could tell by her wife's breathing that she was fuming—and pouting. After about twenty minutes of listening to Cordelia's irritated, sleepless sighs, Aubrey took her left hand and rhythmically rubbed her wife's back in a circular motion like one would do to an infant trying to soothe it to sleep. At first, all Cordelia could feel was the coolness of her wife's wedding band on her bare back, but eventually, she drifted off to sleep like the child that she was.

* * *

The next morning, Cordelia was the one who woke up to an empty bed. When she turned over to look for her wife, she found only *The Fellowship of the Ring* sitting atop Aubrey's pillow.

While it was a Monday, and usually a workday for her, it was also Boxing Day, which in England is a national holiday. As such, she could not expect Clark to drive her to the Wainwright, and she had no desire to spend the day with the *three witches of Macbeth*: Beatrice, Miranda, and Aubrey. This left only Ophy since Portia was spending the holidays with Roy and their friends in Sussex.

After loudly knocking on her daughter's door, Cordelia found Ophy smartly dressed in a short red-and-gold floral print Burberry wrap dress and wearing thigh-high black suede boots.

"Why are you dressed like you're about to work the streets of St. Albans at such an early hour, Darling?" Cordelia asked in apparent disdain and horror.

"I'm going shopping with Robby in town," Ophy matter-of-factly answered her.

Robby, of course, was the seventeen-year-old bloke who had been permitted to touch her daughter's breasts, and *God only knows what else*.

"Is it not a bit early in the day for...such attire?" Cordelia asked as she warily scanned Ophy's outfit. *She looks like a high-priced prostitute.*

"We're going to the Ritz for lunch after we go to Harrods."

"At the Ritz hotel?" Cordelia uncomfortably asked.

Ophy would be sixteen in ten days, and thanks to her incessant obsession with listening to parenting podcasts about teenage sexuality, Cordelia knew that this was right about the time that young girls started allowing boys to touch more than their breasts.

Ophy smirked. "Yep."

While 'yep' was an innocent and simple enough answer, all Cordelia heard was, especially with Ophy's wardrobe choice: *After the crepe suzette downstairs, I'm getting fucked upstairs.*

"Right, well, isn't there a more appropriate place for teenagers to eat? Harrods has several excellent restaurants, doesn't it?"

"Yes, but I asked Robby to take me to the Ritz as both my Christmas and birthday presents—since he'll be away skiing while I'm *forced* to stay here," Ophy said insolently.

Surely she wouldn't give up her innocence over something so fucking petty?

"I don't—"

But before Cordelia could finish saying, 'want you going to any goddamn fucking hotel with a teenage bloke,' Aubrey appeared out of nowhere.

"Robby's waiting for you in the foyer, Ophelia." Aubrey could see by the furious look on her wife's face that she had interrupted a tense conversation. *Cordy looks like she's going to implode.* "Is everything all right?"

Mother and daughter looked stonily at one another, daring the other to say something.

There are just some things that you don't say to anyone, let alone your teenage daughter—Cordelia had not learned this vital life lesson in her thirty-five-and-a-half years and bitterly said, "Apparently, she has chosen to slag her way across the sheets of the Ritz instead of the slopes of Switzerland. Don't use my fucking Black Card to pay for it, please."

"Cordy!" Aubrey shouted, outraged.

Ophy looked as though she'd been slapped across the face. But, although she didn't know it quite yet, she'd not only inherited her mother's stunning good looks but her unrelenting need to hide her true feelings behind spite.

"At least I don't hide whom I'm fucking, you closeted dyke!"

Ophy hastily grabbed her black Louis Vuitton clutch, which Cordelia had given her for Christmas, jerked out the Black Card in question, and handed it to her mother as she walked out the door without another word.

When Aubrey came toward her completely devastated wife and attempted to hug her, Cordelia knocked her arms aside and sidestepped her. Then, she, too, walked out of her daughter's bedroom without another word.

* * *

In the past, when her unwise decisions came back to haunt her, Cordelia took an extra Prozac and a couple more Valium to cope. But now that Aubrey controlled her pills *like Nurse Ratched*, Cordelia turned to drink—vodka in LA and wine in St. Albans.

Beatrice and Aubrey could gauge how upset and/or unhappy Cordelia was by how many glasses of wine she drank at dinner. One to two glasses meant slightly; three to four meant moderately; and five or more meant that she should be given an extra Prozac and taken directly to bed.

After the blow-up in Ophy's room that morning, no one saw Cordelia until dinnertime. Apparently, she'd not spent the day in her bedroom pouting—where Aubrey had looked for her numerous times throughout the day—but in the Wainwright wine cellar.

First, she was twenty minutes late for dinner—Cordelia was never late for anything, especially not dinner. Second, her black Barbour slacks were wrinkled and covered in dust—Cordelia was always immaculately dressed and pressed. Third, she brought an open bottle of Pinot Grigio to the table with her, where she plopped down in her chair in between her mother and wife and drank straight from the bottle—Cordelia would never put her mouth on something that had not been sterilized first—except Aubrey, of course. Fourth, when Flora hastily brought her dinner plate, she pushed it back—Cordelia always ate every bite of whatever English food was before her—even Aubrey's horrible Christmas dinner from years ago.

After a few moments of stupefied silence and startled stares of disbelief passed across the table, Beatrice finally said, "Perhaps you should join Portia in Sussex, Darling. Apparently, you'd fit right in with her crowd."

"Yes, Mother."

This was followed by another swig straight from the bottle.

"Should I ask Miranda to go fetch one of Desi's bottle nipples for you, then?" Beatrice bitingly asked.

"Yes, Mother, it might be the only nipple I have in my mouth for quite some time," Cordelia caustically answered.

At this precisely aimed dig directed at her, Aubrey slammed her hand down on the table and then attempted to grab the wine bottle from her wife's hands.

"Give me that fucking bottle now, you spoiled, pouting child!" Aubrey shouted as she struggled with Cordelia's vice grip on the neck of said bottle.

And, then, something happened that had never taken place in all their years together; Cordelia took her free left hand and roughly shoved Aubrey so hard that she knocked over both her wife and the chair she was seated on onto the floor. Yes, she'd playfully slapped her ass before, and there were times when she'd been less than gentle in bed—especially the last three-and-a-half months—but never had she laid a violent hand on her wife.

Before Miranda and Clark could frantically gather their two daughters to flee the dining room before all hell broke loose, Beatrice stood up from her seat and slapped her eldest daughter resoundingly hard across her right cheek. Then, she roughly grabbed Cordelia's chin and jerked her face back toward her own, which was towering menacingly above her daughter's.

"Do I need to have you locked away again?"

"I'm married now, Mother, so you can't. And, thankfully, at least one of my spouses—I'm like a Mormon now, Mother, and you thought I'd end up a lonely cat lady—needs me," Cordelia slurred.

By this time, Aubrey had regained an upright standing position but not a position of understanding of what exactly her wife and mother-in-law were referring to.

"What the fuck are you talking about?"

A sinister laugh bellowed off the dining room walls, and Cordelia wagged an uncoordinated finger at her mother. "Oh, my, Mother, haven't you told your closest confidant that she's married to a *crazy* bitch? And people say I'm the liar."

Then Cordelia attempted to take another swig from the bottle, but before she could bring it to her mouth, Beatrice slapped her again, which jarred the bottle loose from her hand and onto the floor.

Beatrice looked as though she might strangle Cordelia at any minute. "*That* is not why you were committed, and you know it! No one has ever called you 'crazy'—no matter how many bloody times you have acted it!"

Aubrey just stared at them both in disbelief. *What else don't I fucking know?*

"I can't deal with…" she paused and disgustedly looked at her beyond drunk wife and irate mother-in-law, "*this*, right now," and walked out of the room.

"Goodnight, *My Love*…enjoy your fucking book!" Cordelia yelled after her and reached across the table for an open bottle of wine sitting atop it. "Let's have another drink, Mummy."

While it had been *many* years since Beatrice had seen her daughter so wholly wasted, she remembered that trying to talk to her when she was was futile. So, instead of berating her daughter, she leaned down and kissed Cordelia's forehead.

"Mummy has had quite enough for tonight, Darling," and she, too, walked silently out of the dining room.

CHAPTER TWELVE

"Term for Term"

Dec. 26-27, 2015: St. Albans, England

Beatrice stood outside the bedroom door several moments before she knocked. She needed time to gather her racing thoughts and mentally prepare herself for the questions she knew Aubrey would want answers to.

How much of the truth did Delia tell her? What if I reveal something that finally pushes this girl away forever—it'll be a crypt and not an asylum that I'll have to worry about...

She softly knocked. "Aubrey...Dear, it's Beatrice."

No 'come in' was issued, but instead, the sound of a lock turning. When the door opened, she saw a half-packed suitcase on the bed and the resolute face of her soon-to-be ex-daughter-in-law.

"Hmm...I thought we might have a chat and a drink—or the whole bottle. Why should Delia have all the fun?" Beatrice began, holding up an unopened bottle of 1800 with two Waterford crystal tumblers stacked atop its lid.

"Um, I'll take the tequila, but you can keep the glasses...and the 'chat,'" Aubrey said as she stepped aside to let Beatrice in.

Beatrice handed her the bottle and made her way over to the bed, where she used her free hand to slide the suitcase over. "I'll take mine in a glass, Dear," she said as she sat and held out her glass.

Aubrey opened the bottle, took a healthy swig for herself, and then poured her mother-in-law a small shot, but Beatrice tilted the glass up, indicating that she wanted...no, needed more.

"Going somewhere—without your wedding ring, nonetheless, Dear?" Beatrice began as she pointed her tumbler toward Aubrey's naked left hand.

"I put it back where it belongs—in her drawer of 'regrets,'" Aubrey said bitterly.

Beatrice weakly smiled, remembering the first time they'd had a meaningful conversation with one another in this very room. "I'm afraid that drawer isn't big enough to hold all of them." Then she drank the entire glass of tequila and looked Aubrey squarely in the eyes. "Ask me whatever you want, Dear, since it appears there's nothing left to lose now."

"Um, we're well past the point of explanations—which should have come from *her* years ago."

"Well, yes, but...if you've *finally* had enough, I want to ensure that when you leave here, you do it knowing the whole truth. I feel it's the least I owe you for putting up with Delia for so long when any other woman would have left her ages ago."

Beatrice then got up, moved the suitcase to the floor, sat back down, and patted the bed. *"If circumstances lead me, I will find Where truth is hid, though it were hid indeed Within the centre."*

Aubrey smiled and sat. "So, she should have been cast as Hamlet instead of Ophelia?"

"Well, Dear, *both*—they were both insane, just for very different reasons," Beatrice quipped. "I'll start...what did she tell you about how Ophy came to be?"

"Um, nothing..."

Beatrice was flabbergasted. "What do you mean 'nothing'? Didn't you ask? Good heavens, if Henry had told me after seven years of marriage that he had a secret daughter, I would've killed him and then bloody interrogated his dead body!"

"That's not how—" Aubrey began.

But Beatrice quickly cut her off. "Nonsense! That was your first mistake! Have you learned nothing after living with her for so long? Delia *must* be forced to do what she doesn't want to do—she's a petulant, hard-headed child who *must* have her own way at all costs. That is *exactly* how Ophy was conceived and how Delia became the person that she is today!"

And, so Aubrey learned the whole disturbing, ugly truth about what her wife did to first become Ms. Wainwright and then a nineteen-year-old mother who abandoned her infant child after being committed as a psychiatric patient, which was followed by a sham marriage to a gay werewolf for half a decade before she met and fell in love with the one person that could save her from herself.

* * *

The following morning, Aubrey found Cordelia passed out on the dining room table wrapped up in a soiled linen tablecloth, with broken Wedgwood china and Waterford crystal littered all across the floor. Aubrey went into the kitchen and found Flora pacing the floor.

"Ms. Aubrey, I don't know what to do. It's breakfast time, but she's made a mess I can't possibly tidy up without waking her."

"Why don't you take the morning off, Flora. The family can fend for themselves, and I promise that *mess* will be cleaned up by lunch," Aubrey said, turning on the cold water of the faucet sink and placing a glass pitcher underneath it. Once the pitcher was filled, she turned off the water and returned to the dining room, promptly pouring its contents over Cordelia's head.

She woke up instantly.

"What the fuck!" Cordelia yelled as she struggled to untangle herself from the tablecloth.

"Good morning, *mi amor*," Aubrey cheerfully said as she sat at the table.

By the look of bewilderment on her face, it was obvious Cordelia had no recollection of how she had come to be where she was.

"You are quite a mess this morning, *mi amor*." Aubrey broadly smiled at the horrified look on Cordelia's face when she looked at her dirty, wrinkled clothing and then at the thousands of pounds worth of broken china and crystal on the wood floor below her. "I think you need a shower and a fresh set of clothes. And, your poor teeth and gums must be going through withdrawal from not being thoroughly brushed, flossed, and disinfected with Listerine last night—plus, it looks like you may have been sick on that tablecloth, too."

Cordelia uneasily ran her hand through her wet hair and used her tongue to inspect her dirty teeth.

Aubrey stood and held out her hand to help her wife down off the table. When she was safely standing and no longer entangled in the tablecloth, Aubrey leaned in and kissed her lightly on the forehead.

"Now, off you go. I'll clean this up, and then we're going to have a nice chat in our bedroom afterward."

* * *

When Aubrey finally finished cleaning up Cordelia's colossal mess in the dining room, she found her freshly showered and fully dressed.

"You look *much* better now, *mi amor*," Aubrey said as she handed her four Ibuprofen, one 60mg Prozac, and a glass of water.

When Cordelia took the proffered pills and water, she noticed Aubrey's naked left hand. "Where's your wedding ring?" she asked hesitantly before swallowing her pills.

Aubrey didn't answer but walked over to the black, gold-inlaid desk and opened its middle drawer. She then took the ring out, walked back over to Cordelia, and held out her right palm, where the ring rested flat in her hand.

"I'm going to speak, and you're going to listen, got it? Nod your head if you understand."

Cordelia nodded apprehensively.

"I've probably loved you from the first moment you told me how *desperately* you wanted me, *mi amor*. I have endured more than any woman should ever be expected to put up with. You are rude, insensitive, ungrateful, selfish, stubborn, and childish. You have withheld affection and, most importantly, the truth from me more times than I can count. These last four months, you have treated my body like a blow-up doll, and last night, you put your hands on it in anger—"

"I'm—" Cordelia interrupted.

But Aubrey quickly and quietly cut her off, "I'm not done speaking, Cordy."

When Cordelia nodded, Aubrey continued.

"Your mother told me *everything* last night that you should've told me years ago. I know *everything* now, Cordy...and while it hurts me more than I could ever explain that I had to hear the truth from her and not you, I still love you and want to spend the rest of my life with you and all of your fucked up issues. But, Cordy, you *must* finally stop *acting* like an adult and *finally* become one. Do you understand?"

Through her tears, Cordelia dutifully nodded.

Aubrey then held out her right hand. "So, these are the terms of our marriage from now on, or this ring goes back in that drawer, and I walk out of your life *forever*.

"First, there will be no more secrets between us. Second, you will stop drinking—except you may have one drink on holidays and special occasions. Third, you will never put your hands on me in anger again. Fourth, which piggybacks off three, you will never violate the sanctity of our bed again by mistreating my body because you are upset with me, and there will be no more pouting or withholding of sex as a form of punishment. Fifth, you will ask Bradley for a divorce so we can finally live our lives openly. Sixth, we will have a baby of our own. Seventh, you *will* and *must* tell Ophy that you are her mother. There is no way that either *we* or *you* can survive if you don't.

"Do you understand me?"

"But Aubrey—" Cordelia pleaded.

"No buts, *mi amor*. Those are my terms," Aubrey resolutely stated. Then she waited for Cordelia to remove the ring from her right palm and place it on her left hand.

Cordelia felt as though she might be sick at any moment, and, then finally, she didn't feel as though but actually knew that she was, so she made a beeline for the toilet. Aubrey followed her into the bathroom and held her hair back from her face as she retched and retched until there possibly couldn't be anything left in her stomach. Then Cordelia sat on the floor with her back against the bathtub while Aubrey wet a towel for her sweat-covered face. As Aubrey dabbed at the perspiration, Cordelia contemplated what she would say next.

There must be some compromise in any marriage.

"*My Love*, I will immediately, and more than willingly, agree to your first four terms…but the other three will take some time. I cannot just drop Bradley to fend for himself. If it were not for him, I would probably be dead.

"As for us having a baby, I am unable to have any more children, so that would rest solely on you. And, until I can work out in my mind how to explain to Ophy that I have been lying to her for sixteen years and then deal with what comes afterward, I am not sure how well she might take it that I abandoned her as an infant but that I am now willing to raise one with you."

Aubrey knew her wife was being earnest with her—she'd not used one single contraction in her counteroffer.

"How long, Cordy?"

"By this time next year, I promise. You will only be thirty-two and still capable of totally ruining your firm ass and sexy legs to bring another germ-infested, messy child into an already overpopulated planet," Cordelia joked. Then she suddenly remembered why she was having a life-altering conversation while sitting beside a toilet on a bathroom floor. "What time did Ophy come home last night?"

Aubrey grinned. "Why—are you worried about having a grandbaby and a baby that are the same age?" But when Cordelia looked as though she might vomit again, Aubrey alleviated her fears by saying, "Don't worry, *mi amor*. I spoke to her this morning, and she assured me that she is still pure as the driven snow… Speaking of snow, Beatrice told her that she could go skiing with her friends."

"She did what?" Cordelia shouted. "In what world does she think it's a good idea to send a teenage girl off on a trip with her boyfriend? Didn't she learn anything from her lackadaisical parenting with Portia? And who the fuck is paying for this?" Cordelia ranted as she struggled to get up off the floor.

Aubrey took pity on her and helped her to her feet. Then she put her arms around her wife's neck, looked into her icy-blue eyes and said, "I'm paying for the trip—I knew you would need time to…process…how to tell her the truth. And, it doesn't matter if *it* happens on a ski trip, at a hotel, or against a black desk, *mi amor*, one day *it* will happen. All you can do, which you have already ridiculously and traumatically done, is prepare her for it."

Cordelia looked skeptical but, at the same time, relieved that Aubrey's arms were around her neck, which possibly meant that she was willing to wait for her last three demands to be met.

"Shall I put your wedding ring back onto your left hand, then— where it shall remain forever without question, Sweetheart?"

Aubrey seductively smiled at her. "On two conditions. First, you need to brush your teeth because your breath is atrocious. Two, I then want you to prove that you fully and *thoroughly* understand Term Four for the rest of the day."

"Are you sure you would not *prefer* to read your book instead?" Cordelia quipped as she reached for her toothbrush.

Aubrey walked backward from her toward their bedroom. "Don't spend forever flossing, *mi amor*; you might miss that sexy librarian you've got the hots for."

After the quickest brushing of her teeth ever recorded, Cordelia found Aubrey lying on their bed wearing only glasses and her wedding ring. Cordelia lecherously eyed every inch of her wife's body.

"My God, you're sexy…Right, how would the sexy librarian like Mrs. Wainwright to enter her depository first?"

Aubrey bit her lip so as not to laugh at Cordelia's inept sexual innuendo. "Mrs. Wainwright just *desperately* wants *her* Cordy to make love with her—*preferably* as slowly and gently as possible, and like there is nothing between them anymore."

* * *

June 2016: St. Albans, England

When Aubrey and Cordelia returned to St. Albans for their summer holiday, only one of Aubrey's final three terms was met: Bradley had been asked to file for divorce under whatever pretense he wished.

At first, Bradley had been resistant to letting his closet friend and beard go, but when Cordelia explained that she must be free to live her life openly with her wife, he reluctantly agreed. However, it was decided that the papers would not be filed until after what he assumed would be his last Christmas blockbuster as Lucien the Lycan. While the idea of waiting until January 2017 to announce the divorce didn't sit well with Aubrey, she also reluctantly agreed when Cordelia reminded her that had it not been for Bradley's romantic meddling, they would've probably never gotten together in the first place. To sweeten the deal, he offered to be their sperm donor once they were ready to start IVF.

Aubrey was more than ready to take him up on his offer, but one last pesky detail needed to be addressed first: Ophelia. When she'd returned from her ski trip in January, mother and daughter made up, and everything was almost entirely right in the Wainwright household.

After much discussion between the wives and Beatrice, it was decided that Ophy would not be told the truth until she finished her final term at St. Mary's, as it would be completely unfair to ruin her last term of secondary school—not to mention it seemed rather cruel to tell her that she'd been lied to her entire life and then be sent back to Cambridge for four months to deal with such a betrayal on her own.

So, how does someone admit the truth when the truth, in general, is what that person has evaded most of their life at all costs? It took Cordelia twenty-eight years to accept that she needed physical and emotional intimacy with another person—not that she was sexually attracted to women—she'd known that since she was a teenager.

While her mother and Bradley had drawn the map and paved the road that led to her bedroom that third Saturday night in September of 2008, it was Aubrey's sheer, bold determination to drive her to the very edge of a cliff from which she had only two options: one, push away from what she feared and fall into a canyon of loneliness forever; two, pull towards what she needed and climb out of an abyss of her own making, which irrevocably not only changed her life but in all likelihood saved it.

* * *

After a sleepless night of rehearsing her own personal Soliloquy of Truth, Cordelia silently studied Aubrey's face as she peacefully slept beside her.

It was their first wedding anniversary, and while it hadn't always been a happy year, it was the most important one of her life. There were no secrets between them, and for the first time in their life together, Cordelia could confide in Aubrey about all of her regrets.

What did I ever do to deserve you?

Aubrey was beautiful, both inside and out. She was patient, kind, generous, and loving.

No woman deserves to be happy more than she does.

Quite simply, she made Cordelia human, an adult, and as close to *normal* as she would ever be.

"Why are you watching me sleep, *mi amor*?" Aubrey groggily asked, opening her eyes to see her wife's icy blue eyes staring at her.

"Because it is the only time when I am not being told what to do," Cordelia joked.

Aubrey laughed seductively. "You get off on being bossed around. 'Cordy, please go slower…Cordy, please go deeper…Cordy, please come already.'"

"*My Love*, you are *never* that polite in bed." Cordelia smirked. "It is more like," Cordelia switched her voice to imitate Aubrey's raspy one, "'Cordy, my pussy isn't a tunnel for a fucking freight train…Cordy, put your tongue inside of me like you fucking mean it…Cordy, for fuck's sake, come in my mouth already; I promise I won't kiss you afterward.' Which, by the way, is always a lie," Cordelia reminded her with a disapproving, though playful, look.

For once, Aubrey was speechless. Never in their close to eight years together had her wife spoken so obscenely to her—it was both repulsive and arousing at the same time.

"Um, so, you do know how to talk dirty then?"

"Of course, *My Love*…I have been fucking you for enough years to know all of the *naughty* words," Cordelia said with a smile as she flipped the comforter over and began to get out of bed.

Aubrey grabbed at her arm in *desperation* to stop her. "Don't you fucking dare go take a shower now!"

"As much as I would love nothing more than to satisfy your wanton desires, Sweetheart, I have very important things to do this morning—and your wet pussy is not at the top of the list." Cordelia laughed as she walked toward their bathroom.

"Cordy!" Aubrey shouted in frustration—and probably shock—as she watched her wife enter the bathroom. "Do you know it's our wedding anniversary?" she pleaded.

At this question, Cordelia leaned out over the doorframe, mischievously smiled, and said the absolute most shocking thing she would ever say in their entire married life. "Has it *only* been a year, then? Hmm…well, perhaps, *My Love*, my tongue can vigorously clean your apparent *desperation* away in the shower."

They'd had sex against a desk, on a couch—the cheerful colored one, not the *so, so, so white* one—and in a bed, but *never* in a shower, which was Cordelia's *Palace of Cleanliness* and not pleasure.

"Who are you? And, where have you been for eight years?" Aubrey asked in disbelief, throwing back the covers as fast as she could.

"This morning, Mrs. Cordelia Wainwright will be assuming the role of Whore Number Two, and then by the end of breakfast, she'll be taking over the role of Mother Number One."

* * *

When they walked into the dining room for breakfast, where Beatrice, Portia, and Miranda were already seated, every pore on Aubrey's face was glowing—not so much Cordelia, who was grimacing.

Beatrice looked at her daughter's noticeable labored gait and asked, "Is there something wrong with your legs, Darling?"

"I...must have pulled something in the shower, Mother," Cordelia uncomfortably answered as she sat in her chair.

"Hmm...well, happy anniversary nonetheless. Tell us, Dear, what rude gift did she give you to mark the special occasion?" Beatrice asked her daughter-in-law.

Aubrey's face burned red, and she giggled like a schoolgirl when she answered. "A *hottttttt* shower."

Portia and Miranda burst into laughter, and Beatrice looked at a glowering Cordelia with both awe and pity.

"Put a folded towel underneath your knees next time, Darling."

"Next time for what?" Ophy asked as she joined them at the table.

"Never you mind," Cordelia quickly answered. Then she looked at Portia and nodded to signal that she was ready to commence the scenario they'd worked out to tell Ophy the truth.

Portia, the irresponsible sister that she was, had gotten herself knocked up and was now seven months pregnant. Beatrice was hopeful that a child would calm her wildness down, but she was also outraged that her youngest daughter refused to get married even when *that cad*, Roy, asked her.

"Well, it looks like we'll have yet another Wainwright girl, Mother," Portia started.

"That's wonderful news, Darling!" Beatrice feigned surprise like the skilled actress that she was.

Next, it was Aubrey's turn. "Um, do you have any names picked out?"

"Goneril, of course," Portia answered matter-of-factly.

Ophy scoffed at this and rudely asked, "What kind of name is that, Portia? Isn't there a better Shakespearean name you can stick her with?"

Cordelia took a long, deep breath, ran her hands through her strawberry-blond hair, and pointedly looked at her daughter with her icy-blue eyes. "All Wainwright women name their daughters after the roles they played when their daughters were conceived, *Ophelia.*"

While Ophy had not exactly inherited her mother's gift with numbers, even she could do this simple math problem. Beatrice was forty years old when Ophy was born, which meant that she was far too old to play a depressed teenage girl on stage. Yet, Dilly was just nineteen when she won her Oscar for playing Ophelia.

Ophy looked disbelieving from one woman to the next, seated around the table. The stoic looks on their faces told her that she had done the math correctly.

"But you're a fucking lesbian! How's that even possible?"

"First, young ladies do not use language like that at the dining table, nor do they use it in front of their aunts, grand-mama, or mothers," Cordelia gently scolded her daughter. "Second, I told you last summer that I was not completely ignorant when it came to men—granted, your conception certainly confirmed that I most assuredly *preferred* women."

"But you're Dilly? How could you—how could *all* of you—lie to me my entire life?" Ophelia's questions were filled with outrage at their betrayal of her.

"Do not blame them for my mistakes, Darling. Portia and Miranda were just girls like yourself when I begged Mama to raise you—I assure you, she did it *most* unwillingly. It is I alone who bears the blame for this ridiculous melodrama. So, if you must hate someone, it should be me."

"But why...why did you do it?" Ophy asked with disbelief in her voice.

"That is an excellent question, Inspector Holmes. Shall I give you my confession now?"

Part IV

Cordelia

CHAPTER THIRTEEN

"Delia"

April-July 1999: St. Albans & Los Angeles, CA

Cordelia Anne Wainwright lived in an insulated world constructed by her various *peculiarities* and her mother's overbearing protection for nearly nineteen years. While she may have spent months away from her parents at boarding school, at least Miranda was there, too. They may not have gotten on well together, but they were still sisters, and, as such, Cordelia could rely on Miranda to step in when her various anxieties and *afflictions* spiraled out of control.

When this happened—way too often—Miranda would ring home and tell their mother that she should 'visit' Cambridge. She never needed to explain why. And, so, Beatrice would drive eighty-plus kilometers on a Sunday and take Cordelia into hand. An hour's drive is easily accomplished—an eleven-and-a-half-hour plane ride, covering a distance of over 8,000 kilometers, is an entirely different matter altogether.

Her departure from St. Albans to Los Angeles would have been worrisome enough for her mother, given Cordelia's history of homesickness, anti-social behavior, and overall fear of the unknown—most particularly strangers, germs, and bacteria—but Beatrice now had to also be concerned about how her daughter would deal with what she—not Cordelia, though—categorized as rape.

Beatrice didn't care how Cordelia compartmentalized what had transpired in Grant's office; to her, any forty-five-year-old man that would use his power—both professionally and physically—to force a naïve virgin to submit to his will was a rapist. As if the act was not enough, Cordelia would now have to deal with him on set for over three *hideous* months and another two films afterward.

It had taken all of Beatrice's British fortitude not to kill *that bastard* the night that she saw the outline of his villainy on her daughter's right shoulder. Had it not been for the fact that she still had two children to raise—Portia, aged fourteen, and Delia, forever aged eight—she would have gladly rid the world, and young actresses everywhere, of Grant Andrews.

Instead, she *visited* him in his office the next day and told him in no uncertain terms that if he ever laid another hand on Cordelia, she would 'end him.' The look in her burning blue eyes told him that she meant every word and demand that she issued.

And, so two days after her daughter's innocence was violated, Beatrice begrudgingly dropped Cordelia at Heathrow with the following instructions: "I will ring you at seven every Sunday morning—you *will* answer. There is to be no drinking or overmedicating—Mummy is not going to be there to take care of you if you do something stupid. And, I expect, there are many pretty, young, dark-haired lesbians with legs for days and firm bottoms in Hollywood. So, if, and *when*, one of them dares to speak to you, for the love of God, Delia, respond like a normal human being."

While Beatrice had done her best to push Cordelia out of her fortified and isolated shell of existence, she knew it wasn't nearly enough to prepare her daughter for a world outside St. Albans, the Wainwright, or St. Mary's.

Beatrice was confident that her intensive tutoring had adequately prepared her daughter for performing on a Hollywood set. However, acting like she knew how to function in the world of reality was a completely different thing. Dr. Stewart had warned Beatrice several times that sheltered children do not typically grow up to be well-adjusted adults, and if there ever was a poster child for arrested development, it was Cordelia. Beatrice, of course, thought she knew best.

Per Beatrice's demands, Grant paid for Cordelia to reside in a suite at the Beverly Wilshire Hotel—on the lowest floor possible, *just in case*. Obviously, her rooms and linens were to be cleaned thoroughly daily.

Since Cordelia didn't drive, he also paid for a chauffeur—the same one, every day—to exclusively transport her to and from the hotel and set—of course, she went nowhere else.

And her food didn't come from the hotel's over-priced, modern American menu, but instead was delivered every day from The Cat & Fiddle Pub & Restaurant, who had every savory pie she liked, as well as sausage rolls, beef Wellington, and, most importantly, sticky English toffee and bread and butter puddings.

And, finally, her new black, tailored everything wardrobe came from Barbour and was purchased on Grant's Black Card.

So, Cordelia had been wrong—on so many levels—about how much a young girl's innocence was worth. His violation of Beatrice's oldest daughter cost Grant exceedingly more than £750,000. It also cost Cordelia the unique experience of having to fend for herself and live like an actual adult who spoke to housekeepers, drove herself places, ordered her own food—or God forbid, ate something other than English food—and picked out her own clothing.

Her mother could do everything for her except function in a world without family or friends. In Los Angeles, all Cordelia did was work, which she was exceptional at. Aubrey would be right some sixteen years later when she said, 'No one takes direction better than Cordelia Wainwright.'

While the smell of Grant's Polo cologne made her nauseous, his pinpoint-focused direction made her a better actress than she would've ever become at the Wainwright. He not only taught her that she most assuredly didn't ever want to have sex with a man again but also how to perform for a camera and not, thankfully, a live audience. When she 'flubbed' a line or missed a mark, there was this beautiful thing called a retake. And, if ever there was a person who needed multiple retakes, it was Ms. Cordelia Anne Wainwright: superbly capable actress/supremely inadequate adult.

* * *

July 1999: St. Albans & London, England

When Cordelia returned to St. Albans in late July, Beatrice was beyond relieved. First, because her daughter hadn't taken a fistful of 'happy pills' and drowned herself in a bathtub. Second, she'd put weight on—when you weigh nothing in the first place, every ounce shows—and her skin was glowing and had never looked more, dare she say it, *radiant.*

Upon first seeing Cordelia, Beatrice thought her daughter had lied to her during their Sunday morning chats when she told her she went nowhere other than to work.

Surely, she has finally met someone she fancies!

This often prayed-for scenario was soon replaced by a most unpleasant realization when her daughter arrived late every morning for breakfast for a week, looking as though she were recovering from a hangover, and, then, most suspiciously, had absolutely no appetite for Mrs. Holt's cooking—even English toffee scones! Of the two possible explanations for all of these changes in her daughter's appearance and behavior—addiction or pregnancy—Beatrice wasn't sure which one would be the easiest to treat.

As they drove alone into London to presumably meet Henry for lunch, Beatrice cautiously asked her daughter what she dared not ask in front of her sisters.

"Delia...Darling, you would tell Mummy if you weren't feeling...well, right?" Beatrice tried her best to keep a tranquil tone and not like she was interrogating her.

"I feel as well as I always do, Mother. I have thrown up quite a lot these last few months, but nothing more than I did when I was performing at the Wainwright. I expect it may be an occupational hazard," Cordelia rationally explained.

"Yes...but...you've been home for over a week, Darling. *Why* might you still be doing it? Surely, you've watched enough documentaries on the human body to know that it isn't normal to be sick every morning for *no* reason," Beatrice asked, turning her head away from the road to look directly at her daughter.

This question sounded off alarm bells for Cordelia, who anxiously asked, "You don't think I have cancer, do you, Mother?"

This panicked question answered Beatrice's own. Had Cordelia been drinking and overmedicating again, she wouldn't have automatically assumed that her body had been infected with a malignant bacteria that would bring about her eventual excruciating death.

Beatrice shook her head exasperatedly at her completely clueless daughter and calmly said, "I don't think it's cancer that has invaded your body, Darling, but perhaps we should be sure."

So, instead of meeting Henry for lunch, Beatrice drove Cordelia to her gynecologist's office—her intended destination when they left St. Albans that afternoon.

* * *

Since Beatrice rightly assumed her daughter's predilections were towards the fairer sex, there had been no need to put her on birth control, so Cordelia had never suffered the indignity of placing her ankles in stirrups and having someone poking around in her vagina.

After a quick but oh-so-unpleasant examination and blood test, Beatrice's suspicions were confirmed: her daughter was almost four months pregnant. Why someone so well versed in all things medical hadn't questioned why she'd not had her period since she'd left St. Albans was beyond Beatrice's comprehension. Yet, this was not the conversation that mother and daughter needed to have now.

The Wainwrights were non-practicing Catholics who only went to Mass when someone was baptized, married, or died, and, occasionally, on Christmas and/or Easter. Yet, years of Catholic school instruction had told Cordelia that abortion was a mortal sin—no matter how a child might have been conceived. This is also why she refused to acknowledge what everyone in her family knew—that she was sexually attracted to women. So, when her mother gently suggested that she should consider terminating the pregnancy, Cordelia vehemently refused.

Beatrice tried to calmly reason with her intransigent daughter. "Darling, Mummy loves you, so I take no joy in saying this, but you are not emotionally equipped to take care of yourself, let alone a child."

But Cordelia, like so many times before and after this conversation, refused to listen to her mother's wise counsel.

"I am already...*different*, Mother. And, because of *it*, I will never marry or have another opportunity to have a child. I am certain that I can learn to be more independent and you can help me when I...struggle with the other bits."

Since she hadn't yet learned how to take care of herself in nineteen years—namely, suspecting there was a reason that she'd not had a period in months or that it wasn't normal to be nauseous nearly every morning for three months—Beatrice was not instilled with much confidence in her daughter's own belief that she could miraculously grow up in just over five short months. Yet, the slim possibility that having a child of her own might finally make Cordelia step outside of her sterilized bubble and into a world of relative normalcy was too tempting of an offer for Beatrice, and so she supported her daughter's choice.

* * *

Aug. 1999-Jan. 2000: St. Albans, England

As actresses, the Wainwright women were exceptionally adept at hiding the truth. As such, Henry was completely oblivious as to how his nineteen-year-old lesbian daughter returned home from Los Angeles nearly four months pregnant.

Per Cordelia's adamant request that it not be revealed how she truly came to be cast in Grant's film, Beatrice explained her daughter's *troubling* condition as the result of an ill-advised, drunken one-night stand. His daughter's recent issues with drinking and overmedicating made this lie plausible. What wasn't credible to Henry was his wife's insistence that she believed Cordelia was ready to be a mother. This, of course, was because she didn't think it herself but prayed every night that she would be proven wrong.

Since she was not a particularly religious person by nature, Beatrice needed a backup plan. And, so for the first time in her acting career, she took an extended hiatus from the Wainwright starting at the end of the fall season's first show, *Much Ado about Nothing*, and announced that she would not return to the stage until the beginning of the fall 2000 season.

In Beatrice's mind, this gave her ample time to adequately prepare her fragile daughter for the unpleasantness of her third trimester, as well as just how physically painful having a baby was—Cordelia's pain tolerance was one out of ten, and that was being generous. Then, since the baby was projected to arrive the second week in January, Beatrice would have approximately nine months to teach her daughter how to properly take care of a child. Under no circumstances were her husband and younger daughters allowed to remind her how well she'd shown Cordelia how to properly care for herself in nineteen years.

Once the morning sickness passed, Cordelia's appetite returned with a vengeance. Mrs. Holt could not cook enough meat pies, sausage rolls, or puddings to satisfy her endless cravings. This, in turn, caused her to gain an unhealthy amount of weight, which first led her to develop hypertension and then preeclampsia. Quite simply put, Beatrice's well-thought-out plans to turn her eldest daughter into a somewhat functioning adult were utterly blown to bits by Cordelia's inability to stop acting like an overweight, spoiled child and shoving food down her throat.

When she wasn't eating, she was complaining—and *bloody pouting*—about her head feeling as though it might *fucking explode* and the *goddamn intolerable pain* from the swelling in her hands and feet, not to mention her inability to do what she loved most—sleep.

Beatrice attempted to use reason on a most unreasonable child by explaining that if Cordelia would only listen to the doctors and stop eating salty, rich, and fatty foods, it would assist in reducing some of the 'agonies' of pregnancy.

As if her daughter's now high-risk pregnancy were not enough to contend with, Beatrice had to deal with Grant's people, who wanted to know why Cordelia couldn't give in-person interviews and attend the premiere of her debut film in November.

Grant's people were apparently as *vulgar* as the films he produced because any well-read person familiar with classic literature would have known precisely what Beatrice meant when she said, "Delia is presently indisposed."

For obvious reasons, Grant was to remain just as in the dark about Cordelia's indisposition as Henry was.

Instead of walking the red carpets in Hollywood, Cordelia was forced to walk the Persian rugs of St. Albans to alleviate her backaches, edema, hypertension, and her unbearable mood swings, which fell somewhere between delusional child and absolute bitch. Not even her mother's tacit approval of her performance in 'that complete abomination of Hamlet,' which the Wainwrights viewed in the privacy of their own home, could turn Cordelia's ever-present frown upside down.

By Christmastime, Beatrice thought she might kill her daughter, while Cordelia was convinced that her soon-to-be daughter was most definitely going to murder her. Although she was rarely right about most things in life, Cordelia's premonitions about her impending death at the hands of the 'beastly creature' within her almost came true when Ophy finally emerged one week early on January 5, 2000.

CHAPTER FOURTEEN

"Ms. Wainwright"

Jan. 5-March 13, 2000: St. Albans, England

When they arrived at St. Albans City Hospital, Cordelia's blood pressure was 160/110, as a result of not only her hypertension but also her strident belief that her death was imminent.

As a result, the doctors agreed that the best course of action was to take the child immediately via C-section. Had this procedure not been so dangerous in her daughter's critical condition, Beatrice would have been most happy not to endure hours of Cordelia's screaming at the top of her lungs about how much 'agony' she was in.

Yet, instead of rubbing her forehead deeply with the palm of her hand in an effort not to yell at her daughter that she'd signed up for the 'agony' of childbirth, Beatrice and Miranda found themselves giving their own AB-negative blood to replace the more than three pints of blood Cordelia lost during and after the child was cut from her uterus. It was a miracle she survived.

During her first few days in the hospital, she was heavily sedated, which made it nearly impossible to introduce mother and daughter. For two days, the nurse brought Ophy into Cordelia's room to get the new mother to hold her child, but each time, Cordelia insisted that she was too weak to do so.

Miraculously, Ophy was born healthy, and, as such, on the third day, the hospital released her into Beatrice's care. Before leaving the hospital, Beatrice took the baby into her daughter's room, stood at the foot of the bed, and tried once more to get Cordelia to hold her child.

"Goddamnit, Delia, this child has been waiting for three days to meet her mother. God only knows how long it will take you to be released, so for the love of God, hold her," Beatrice quietly implored her as she carried the baby to the side of the bed.

As she knew this was the only way she would get rid of her mother, Cordelia nodded and watched Beatrice gently place Ophy against her chest.

"Put your hand under her neck, now slide her into the crook of your arm, and put your hand under her bottom," Beatrice instructed.

Once Cordelia had safely cradled Ophy, Beatrice stood back from the bed and watched. She didn't like what she saw. Instead of seeing her daughter shed tears of joy, she saw a look of apprehensive dread cross Cordelia's face.

After less than a minute, Cordelia irritably asked, "How much longer must I do this, Mother, before you leave me in peace? I'm exhausted and need my rest."

For obvious reasons, Beatrice couldn't shake the living hell out of her daughter—she was holding Ophy, and she had stitches—and scream at the top of her voice, 'the rest of your bloody life'; so, she did what she always did: rubbed her forehead deeply with the palm of her hand.

After she felt she could speak in a tone that wouldn't startle Ophy, Beatrice said, "Motherhood is for life, Delia. It doesn't matter if a child is three days old or nineteen years old; a mother must always be there for her child."

"Well, your child needs you to take this one away so that she can sleep." Cordelia leaned forward, drew Ophy from her chest, and held out her arms.

Beatrice shook her head in disbelief and removed Ophy from her daughter's arms while a very familiar refrain echoed through her mind: *It's just not normal.*

* * *

A mother and child normally stay in the hospital for one to two days after delivery. As she never did anything normally, Cordelia's recovery time from her brush with death was over two weeks—in a *bloody* hospital where all sorts of bacteria and pathogens threatened to invade her weakened immune system.

As such, her anxiety level was already at an all-time high, but her anxiousness was only heightened by the realization that once she left the hospital, a helpless infant awaited her at home. These things, combined with the fact that she received an Oscar nomination on January 13 that caused her nurses to look at her and her chart a little too closely for her liking, only exacerbated an already fraught situation. When Miranda came to fetch her on January 21, sixteen days after the birth of Ophy, Cordelia looked as though she were about to break into a million pieces.

When she entered the house, Cordelia went straight to her bedroom and locked it and the bathroom door adjoined to Miranda's room. Beatrice was beside herself. Not only was she exhausted from taking care of a newborn by herself for thirteen days, but now she had to worry about her oldest daughter's fragile mental state.

No matter how often or loudly Beatrice banged on the locked bedroom door, Cordelia refused to open it. This went on for two days before Beatrice ordered Henry to break down the door. When he did, they found her curled up in a ball, virtually comatose, in bed, mumbling gibberish.

As much as she despised doing it, Beatrice called Dr. Stewart and begged her to come to the house. As if making that call was not enough of a bitter pill to swallow, Beatrice then had to choke on the psychiatrist's diagnosis: postpartum psychosis.

Postpartum psychosis is a rare, life-threatening mental illness that affects 1 in 1,000 mothers. New mothers suffering from it often exhibit obsessive, paranoid, hallucinogenic, delusional thoughts, fluctuate between a manic and depressive state, and suffer from insomnia and appetite loss. However, the most worrisome thing about postpartum psychosis was the possibility of a mother doing harm to herself or her child.

Preferably, it is treated in a specialized mother and baby psychiatric unit, where both mother and child stay. At first, Beatrice was resistant to this prescribed course of action. However, once Dr. Stewart explained studies showed this was their best option for creating a secure, positive attachment between Cordelia and Ophy, Beatrice agreed to commit her daughter.

Cordelia and Ophy entered the Thumbswood Mother and Baby Unit in Hertfordshire on January 22. When Beatrice was permitted to visit mother and child at the facility, she was not encouraged by what she saw.

Cordelia was withdrawn and listless and had little interaction with Ophy. When she did hold Ophy, Cordelia looked as though she were in excruciating pain, and when the baby cried or got fussy in her arms, she would beg Beatrice or the nurse to take the child as far away as possible. She had no interest in feeding or changing Ophy, and when Cordelia wasn't sleeping, she adamantly demanded to go home to her quiet and clean room. No matter how much Beatrice begged her daughter to try harder to connect with Ophy, Cordelia refused.

Once the doctors could say with confidence that Cordelia was not a threat to herself or the baby, they reluctantly released both into Beatrice's promise of constant supervision and care on March 12. When they returned home, Cordelia immediately went to her room, locked the door, and began packing her belongings.

At 9:00 a.m. the following day, a town car arrived to pick Cordelia up and take her to Heathrow Airport. This was news to Beatrice, whom Cordelia had failed to inform that she was abandoning her two-month-old daughter to return to her film career in Los Angeles.

"Goddamnit, Delia! You cannot drop an infant at my feet as though it was one of your childhood dolls that needs to be tucked away in a toy chest," Beatrice loudly pleaded with her daughter as Cordelia rolled her luggage down the same Persian rugs she'd walked to ease her backaches during pregnancy.

Silence.

Beatrice was livid but more worried about her daughter's fragile state of mind. The most frightening thing Beatrice could imagine was Cordelia traveling over 8,000 kilometers across the world to live alone with no one to look after her.

"Darling, Mummy promised you she would help you, and I intend to do just that. You don't need to run away. We can fix... *this.*"

When they reached the front door, Cordelia turned to her mother and said in a dead-sounding voice, "I cannot be fixed, Mother. I am *different* from other people. You were right; I am not emotionally equipped to care for a child...and, perhaps, myself. But what I am equipped to do, thanks in no small part to you, is act, which is exactly what I intend to do."

As she attempted to walk out the door, Beatrice grabbed Cordelia by the arm, swung her daughter around to face her, and implored her: "Not long ago, I told you that I did my best to teach you right from wrong and that you had to decide for yourself. You didn't listen to me then, but for the love of God, Cordelia, listen to me now: this is *wrong.*"

When Cordelia stared blankly at her impassioned entreaty, Beatrice hugged her as tightly as any mother has ever embraced her child and whispered in her ear, "I love you, Darling. Please don't do this...you will regret it for the rest of your life." Then she brushed Cordelia's hair back from her forehead and kissed it deeply.

There they stood for what seemed like an eternity until finally Cordelia broke her mother's hold on her, stood back, tilted her chin up, and looked determinedly at Beatrice with her tear-filled ice-blue eyes.

"I expect you are right, Mother."

With that, Cordelia walked out the door without another word to her mother. They would not speak to or see one another again for three years.

* * *

March 2000-Feb. 2003: Los Angeles, California

When Cordelia arrived in Los Angeles, her first stop was the Creative Artists Agency. Unbeknownst to Beatrice, her daughter rang Geoffrey from her room in the psychiatric ward and asked him to find her the best talent agent and lawyer available in LA.

Armed with a Best Supporting Actress Oscar and Geoffrey's recommendation, Cordelia marched into Brenda Specter's office and declared that she needed a shark to break her contract with Grant and to help her become one of the most influential actresses in the industry.

After her prolonged stays in the hospital and then on the psych ward, Cordelia was gaunt, pale, and far from radiantly beautiful. However, she was laser-focused and determined, and she had a very powerful friend named Oscar, who convinced Brenda to take her on as a client. Within two weeks, Cordelia had film offers from some of the best directors and producers in the industry.

Since Grant had practically paid for everything the first time she came to LA, Cordelia had most of her £750,000 left. She used it to rent a small studio apartment in Burbank, which she had fumigated and professionally cleaned before moving in. Her furniture consisted of a queen-sized bed and mattress, a black, gold-inlaid pigeonhole desk with a chair, a coffeemaker, and a microwave.

She then had scar revision surgery to remove any traces of her C-section—and her unforgivable abandonment of Ophy.

For close to three years, she did nothing but go to work at the studio, visit the library, shop at the store around the corner from her apartment, listen to audiobooks on her Walkman, and sleep. She had no friends other than vodka, Prozac, and Valium.

She had a cell phone, which only Brenda called, and an address that only her agent and car service knew. She had no contact with her family other than a £10,000 monthly check she had Brenda send to Beatrice and the yearly gold-framed pictures of her family that her mother sent as Christmas and birthday presents to the agent's office. She kept these pictures and her Oscar in her closet along with her black, tailored everything Barbour wardrobe.

In three years, she made eight films and earned another Best Supporting Actress nomination and her first Best Actress nomination. She never attended any parties or award shows, and she did as little press as Brenda could manage to convince the producers of her films that was necessary. In those rare interviews and talk show appearances, she never mentioned that she was a mother and only grudgingly spoke about her family back in England.

Ms. Wainwright's taciturn personality was regarded as British wit. The industry easily overlooked it because she was a highly professional actress who was never late, always knew her lines, and did precisely whatever her director told her. Plus, her dark, depressing films made money and earned and/or won various nominations and awards.

When her male co-stars, and occasionally some of the female ones, showed romantic interest in her, Cordelia politely declined their advances and said she was otherwise attached. Of course, the only 'attachment' that she had was either her hand or vibrator. That is why Cordelia was most unhappy when Brenda suggested that she meet her most famous client, Bradley Simpson.

"I am not presently interested in having a relationship," Cordelia stated matter-of-factly.

Brenda, of course, knew this. Each time she brought up the subject of Cordelia finding someone—*anyone*—to take her to industry parties and award shows she was immediately shut down. But her cash cow, Bradley, had an image problem.

His *Lycan* franchise was worth billions, but his inability to sustain a long-standing heterosexual relationship made him look like a forty-year-old womanizer—and worse, inside the industry as a closeted gay man. To Brenda, it made perfect sense to pair Cordelia with him because she knew Cordelia wouldn't ask any unwanted questions and would be perfectly happy if her 'boyfriend' showed no sexual interest in her whatsoever.

"Neither is he, CW—you're made for one another."

So, at age twenty-two, Cordelia *finally* went on her first 'date' with anyone.

Bradley was handsome, charming, and, most importantly, blunt.

"You don't talk much, do you?" he asked across the table as they scanned their dinner menus.

Cordelia didn't lower the menu before her face when she tartly answered, "You talk enough for the both of us."

This response elicited a thunderous laugh from her dinner 'date.' After a few moments of awkward silence, Bradley tried again. "What do you do for fun?"

"I sleep—*alone*," Cordelia said pointedly as she lowered her menu and fixed her icy-blue eyes on his green ones.

Bradley grinned. "Must get awful lonely..."

"Loneliness is the perfect companion. It neither speaks, expects anything in return, nor makes any demands."

"But what about your...physical needs?" Bradley delicately asked.

Cordelia took a moment to study his handsome but disgustingly bearded face before she answered. While Brenda had not come out and said it, Cordelia knew why their agent insisted they should meet—they were each other's perfect closeted match.

"I am well accustomed to *handling* my own physical needs. As such, I believe you and I could get on quite well together. You may carry on with whomever you like, and I will no longer have to swat away overzealous men."

"But what about the overzealous women?" Bradley quipped.

She did her best not to blush. "I am not interested in them, *either*."

Bradley didn't believe her, but he knew a good thing when he saw it, and Cordelia's stalwart repudiation of all things romantic and/or sexual was the answer to his image problem. She was beautiful, talented, well-spoken, somewhat funny, and more than willing to accept a relationship without physical or emotional intimacy.

"What are you doing next Saturday?"

Thus began the fifteen-year 'romance' between Lucien the Lycan and Ms. Wainwright. Within two months, Cordelia had a $200,000 three-carat fancy intense blue diamond platinum engagement ring to match the color of her ice-blue eyes, and they were cohabitating in the modest four-bedroom ranch-style cornflower blue-brick home in Irvine that Bradley bought for her and also gave her free-reign to decorate however she saw fit—white, *so, so, so white*.

* * *

Bradley was rarely home, and Cordelia liked it that way. He was loud, obnoxious, clumsy, and made lewd suggestions about introducing Cordelia to women who could help her with her irritability and frigidness.

Not unsurprisingly, Cordelia never had visitors to the house. That is why she was surprised when someone knocked on her door on February 23, 2003.

When she opened the door, she found Geoffrey standing outside it.

"If she's sent you to drag me back, you can tell her you didn't find me," Cordelia coolly said as she began to shut the door.

Geoffrey wedged his foot between the door and its frame to prevent this. "We need to have a serious chat, Delia."

"How serious?" Cordelia cautiously asked.

Geoffrey weakly smiled. "*Deathly* serious. Please let me in… this isn't a chat to be had on a doorstep."

With trepidation about what was to come, Cordelia opened the door, stepped aside, and let Geoffrey enter. He was visibly surprised by the overwhelming whiteness of the house—and the half-empty bottle of Grey Goose sitting on the oversized square-shaped coffee table.

When Cordelia saw him look at the bottle, she asked, "Would you like a drink?"

"That sounds like a grand idea...pour yourself one, too."

As Cordelia dispensed the vodka, she motioned her head toward the pristinely white Wynn leather couch. "Have a seat."

Geoffrey sat, but when Cordelia remained standing, he suggested, "Perhaps you should sit, too."

Cordelia handed him his drink and sat as he suggested.

"Obviously, something terrible has happened. Otherwise, the Grim Reaper would not have been dispatched to my door. Just say it already, Geoffrey."

He took a moment to gather his thoughts and to down his drink. "Right, well...there's no easy way to say this, but you *must* come home at once, Delia. Your father died two days ago from an aneurysm. The funeral is the day after tomorrow."

For a moment, his words didn't register in her mind. Henry was only forty-nine years old and in good health.

This can't possibly be right.

But Geoffrey's sympathetic, tear-filled eyes told her that it was true.

"I cannot go home...right now. I have just begun filming my—" she began.

Geoffrey cut her off, "You *must* come home. Your mother is a wreck, and...well, matters concerning the Wainwright need to be dealt with. Beatrice is in no condition to deal with them, and your sisters are...useless regarding such things."

"What sort of matters?" Cordelia asked uneasily.

"Financial ones."

* * *

Feb. 24-March 20, 2003: St. Albans, England

The first thing she heard when she walked in the door was Ophy's animated voice screaming, "Mama, Mama." It felt like vicious pinpricks across every skin cell of Cordelia's body.

As she entered the living room, Cordelia saw her mother sitting on the couch, watching a three-year-old toddler running around. Obviously, Ophy had aged, but Cordelia couldn't help but notice that Beatrice also looked older than the last time they'd seen one another. She had visible crow's feet and lines around her mouth.

When Beatrice saw her, she half-grinned. "I knew that Judas would bring you back."

Ophy looked curiously at Cordelia but didn't speak to her. Instead, she ran to Beatrice, who picked her up and sat her on her lap.

Even though it was only two o'clock in the afternoon, Cordelia walked over to the liquor stand and poured herself an exceedingly full glass of her father's Jameson. Then, she sat in the chair furthest away from Beatrice and Ophy and started drinking.

Beatrice said nothing, but her disapproving eyes said everything. Then, Ophy pointed at Cordelia and asked, "Who?"

This question elicited a bitter laugh from Beatrice. "Who indeed!" She looked directly at Cordelia and asked in a disapproving voice, "Didn't your mother teach you any manners? It is rude not to introduce yourself."

At that, Cordelia stood, emptied her glass of its contents, walked to the couch, and crouched down to make her introduction. There sat the child she had abandoned, quizzically staring down at her with big blue eyes, though not the same icy-blue color as hers. Ophy's hair was thicker than her mother's but the same strawberry-blond shade.

"Hello, Ophy. My name is…Delia." When she said 'Delia,' it sounded like a pained croak.

Beatrice shook her head and narrowed her eyes at her daughter's answer but didn't correct Cordelia's misrepresentation of who she *really* was. Instead, she asked Ophy in a sing-song voice, "Can you say Delia?"

Then it was said. "Dilly! Dilly!" Ophy said excitedly as she grabbed Cordelia's face with her hands.

Cordelia bit the inside of her jaw to control any unwanted signs of weakness and tried not to recoil from Ophy's touch. After a moment that seemed like forever, she slowly drew back, patted her daughter on the head, and said, "Good girl." She then stood upright, returned to the liquor stand, and poured yet another exceedingly full glass of whisky.

"Does it ease your nerves or your conscience, Darling?" Beatrice's question dripped with venom.

Cordelia looked at her mother holding Ophy's squirming body on her lap and answered, "Drink eases my nerves, Mother. Knowing that I have left *her* in your capable hands eases my conscience." Then she drained the glass of its contents and walked out of the room.

* * *

Once Henry was interred in the Wainwright crypt, the two-day silently agreed-upon truce ended. During that time, few words were spoken between mother and daughter; Cordelia consumed many drinks, and Beatrice gave many irritated headshakes.

Cordelia did everything she could to avoid Ophy, but, like any child, she was fascinated by the house's new visitor and was constantly at her mother's side, demanding her attention. Cordelia's deliberate, uncomfortable attempts to dissuade this attention both infuriated and pleased her mother.

"It looks like you have an admirer, Darling."

As the oldest child, Cordelia was familiar with how small children behaved, but Ophy's never-ending chattering, climbing on her legs and lap, and asking of questions were nerve-wracking. She was a ball of energy who wanted to be the focus of everyone in the room—Ophy was the complete opposite of her mother.

To deal with Ophy's exuberance—and her guilt—Cordelia always had a drink in her hand and swallowed Valium like mints. And, when the child was finally put to bed, things only got worse because that's when Beatrice was free to unleash three years of anger and disappointment on her daughter.

"Where's your ring, Darling?" Beatrice derisively asked.

Cordelia had deliberately chosen to leave it back in Irvine.

When her daughter didn't answer, Beatrice continued her assault. "Are we to be invited to the wedding? Perhaps Ophy could be the flower girl. Have you mentioned to your *fiancée* that you have a daughter?"

Silence.

"I'll take that as a no. Is it a happy match, then? I read that he bought you a four-bedroom house…might one of those bedrooms be turned into a nursery anytime soon?" Beatrice pointedly asked.

Cordelia, of course, knew what her mother was *really* asking. "No."

"No to a nursery or no to a happy match?"

"I am quite happy with our relationship, Mother. I don't expect there to be any need for a nursery, especially since the doctors told me that another…attempt to have a child could be dangerous," Cordelia cautiously answered.

"Hmm…so, it's a happy and *healthy* union, then? I must say, Delia, he doesn't seem like *your type*…what with the *beard* and all," Beatrice mercilessly needled her daughter.

Fed up with her mother's game of cat and mouse, Cordelia confirmed what Beatrice already suspected.

"He and I are *alike*, Mother. Which makes our relationship mutually beneficial."

"It might benefit him, Darling, but it's yet one more stone you have paved toward the road to your own destruction."

Variations of this conversation continued for two weeks, along with digs about Cordelia's unconscionable abandonment of her daughter, before Cordelia worked up the courage to address the two issues she'd really come to St. Albans for.

"Mother, the Wainwright is bankrupt. Bradley and I will give you the money to keep it afloat, but you *must* return to the stage. Miranda is not ready to—"

Beatrice cut her daughter's lecture off quickly. "And *who* will take care of Ophy, then?"

"Why do you think I send you money every month? For fuck's sake, Mother, a nanny is not a novel concept to you. You had no issue returning to the stage after you spit us out. Why should this time be any different?" Cordelia heatedly asked.

"Because you and your sisters had a goddamn mother who came home every night and who ate breakfast with you every morning—and who spent your summer holidays and Christmastime with you! Ophy hasn't seen her fucking *mother* in three bloody years!" Beatrice yelled.

"So, I am to be blamed for this?" Cordelia unwisely asked.

"You bloody well should be blamed for something! Whether you will own it is an entirely different matter. How do you sleep at night knowing what you've done, you pathetic excuse for a human being?" Beatrice caustically asked.

At this, Cordelia wearily shook her head. "That's exactly why I left, Mother. I will not make excuses for what I did—it was reprehensible—but I am somewhat better now.

"I have learned these past three years that I can...function on my own. No, that does not mean that I am ready to...fully own up to my responsibility when it comes to Ophy, but if you allow me to help you with the theater and, for God's sake, go back to performing, I will meet you halfway when it comes to Ophy."

Beatrice was both startled and intrigued by Cordelia's admission of her own faults and her willingness to correct them. "How?"

"You will go back to the theater. We will hire a nanny to care for her while you are there. And, every summer and Christmastime, I will come home and...perhaps, after some time, I will be ready to be more than 'Dilly' to her," Cordelia bargained with her mother.

While this was not the exact correction of her daughter's regretful decision that Beatrice wanted to hear, it was a start. After three years of not knowing if Cordelia would ever return and be ready to be a normal person and mother to Ophy, Beatrice greedily grabbed with both hands at this one sliver of hope her daughter offered her.

CHAPTER FIFTEEN

"Dilly"

July-Aug. 2003: St. Albans, England

After a four-month absence, Cordelia returned to St. Albans as Mrs. Bradley Simpson. The wedding ceremony occurred in their living room at the end of June. The only guests were Brenda and a photographer; there was no reception. Cordelia reluctantly agreed to toss aside her usual black for optics and wore a white Oscar de la Renta guipure-lace tweed midi dress. The press was told that the newlyweds went to London for their honeymoon—which they did; after delivering Cordelia to Luton Airport via private jet, Bradley and his current boy-toy flew to the Maldives.

To honor her bargain with Beatrice, Cordelia asked Bradley to front her the money to start her own production company, which she named Willowbrook. It would not only be easier to manage her work schedule if she produced her own films, but it would also be more profitable. Additionally, it allowed her to choose who she worked with, the subject matter of her films, and their overall production value.

Much to her mother's consternation, Cordelia asked Geoffrey to leave the Wainwright and join her at Willowbrook. He would run the company; she would have creative control.

When her mother bristled at the idea of losing Geoffrey to Hollywood—'the cesspool of civilization'—Cordelia smirked. "Just think, Mother, you will not only have Mrs. Holt to spy on me at home, but Geoffrey can keep tabs on me at work, too."

Mrs. Holt, of course, had also been poached from London by Cordelia, who made her an offer so sweet that she couldn't refuse—plus, of all the Wainwrights, Ms. Delia was her favorite: no one praised her food more and was easier to pick up after.

At age twenty-three, Cordelia was her own boss, married, and a renowned actress. To the outside world, she was a well-adjusted, successful young woman. To her mother, she was an emotionally bankrupt, immature child.

How her daughter could manage to play roles that demanded emotional complexity in front of the camera but then be so one-dimensional in reality was utterly puzzling to Beatrice. She often wondered if Cordelia might be a sociopath because she was indifferent, anti-social, narcissistic, and manipulative. Yet, while she kept it hidden well, Cordelia could also be empathetic, gregarious, generous, and heartbreakingly innocent. Her daughter's unyielding need for structure and order—and *bloody cleanliness*—controlled her like an abusive spouse. It also made her poor mother material because children are metaphorically and literally messy.

The first month she was home, Cordelia did everything she could to avoid being left alone with Ophy. Whenever Beatrice attempted to excuse herself from the family's living room without taking Ophy, Cordelia would say, "I am feeling quite tired, Mother. Perhaps I should take a nap."

It didn't matter if it was 10:00 a.m. or 5:00 p.m., Cordelia was always tired—she took more 'naps' than her three-year-old daughter. Beatrice, of course, knew her daughter loved to sleep, but she also understood that Cordelia was petrified of being left responsible for the safety of Ophy.

It didn't help that she was well on her way to being soused by two o'clock daily, either. For someone who'd avoided alcohol like the Plague as a teenager, Cordelia had a particular fondness for it now.

At lunch, Cordelia would start with a glass of wine, and by dinnertime she'd switched to tumblers of vodka. Beatrice had no idea how much Valium Cordelia popped in between drinks, but her glassy ice-blue eyes and lethargic state told Beatrice it was excessive. Under normal circumstances, Beatrice would have outright confronted Cordelia about her drinking and pill-popping. Yet, after her three-year absence from their lives, Beatrice was just glad to have her home—drunk or sober. However, it put a chink in Beatrice's newly formed *Operation Make Cordelia Normal* plan.

During Cordelia's three-week return home following Henry's death, Beatrice studied her closely. Her time in Los Angeles had made her more self-sufficient and confident but also made her colder and, most distressingly, unmanageable.

Beatrice could somewhat bend Cordelia to her will before she ran away from her adult, motherly responsibilities. Yes, she and her various *afflictions* had been challenging to manage, but Cordelia could still be slightly controlled by a stern stare or a cutting suggestion by Beatrice. Now, none of those things affected her. Instead, she poured another drink and/or popped a pill. This new version of Cordelia displeased Beatrice, who *desperately* wanted her daughter to connect with Ophy and not bottles of booze and pills.

By all accounts, according to Geoffrey, who'd returned to America with Cordelia in March to set up Willowbrook, *Ms. Wainwright* was a highly professional, though temperamental actress who was never late and always laser-focused on her job. Yes, she did look a bit haggard on Monday mornings, which Beatrice rightly assumed was because Cordelia passed her lonely, uneventful weekends draining bottles of vodka, but by Tuesday, she was in top form.

So, Beatrice decided to use Cordelia's neurotic need for structure and order against her by suggesting at the end of July that she wasn't quite sure that Geoffrey's nephew Clark was up to the job of running the Wainwright. As Cordelia's money kept the doors of the theater open, Beatrice rightly surmised that she would want to ensure that it wasn't being mismanaged.

So, instead of waking up every morning at well past nine hungover, Cordelia left for town at 8:00 a.m. during the week. Most importantly, she didn't drink during the day and limited herself to two glasses of wine at dinner.

While this situation wasn't ideal for Beatrice's much prayed for bonding experience between her daughter and granddaughter, Cordelia was lucid in the evenings. She interacted with Ophy before she was put to bed at eight-thirty.

For approximately two hours every night, Beatrice watched Cordelia grudgingly sit on the living room floor and play with Ophy, or even more heart-warming, allow the child to squirm in her lap as she struggled to read picture books to her. Yet, under no circumstance would Cordelia allow herself to be left alone with Ophy. Beatrice had a scheme for this as well.

Because Beatrice and Cordelia were home, Ophy's nanny, Ms. Johnson, was given weekends off in the summer. Since she didn't want to overwhelm Cordelia with the prospect of having to take care of Ophy by herself regularly, Beatrice waited until the very last Saturday of her daughter's summer holiday to prove to her that she was capable of keeping a three-year-old alive for an entire day without supervision.

In Cordelia's mind, Saturday mornings were for sleeping in, especially when she drank a bottle of wine on Friday evenings. Yet, instead of waking up at well past nine, she was awakened by gentle hand slaps to the face and exuberant, demanding shrieks of, "Dilly, Dilly, Dilly!"

If starting her morning off being unceremoniously roused by a child in her bed was not enough, that same child was holding a crumbly chocolate biscuit in her non-slapping hand.

Cordelia looked at her mother, standing over her, as though Beatrice had lost her mind. "What the…heck, Mother?"

Highly satisfied with her stealth attack, Beatrice said, "Your sisters and I need to go into town this morning to shop."

"*All* of you?" Cordelia suspiciously asked as she sat up.

"Yes." It was said forcefully and in a tone that told Cordelia it was futile to argue. "We should be home by dinner," Beatrice said as she turned away from the bed and walked toward the door.

"That's ten hours from now, Mother!" Cordelia shouted.

"If you can tell time, you can watch a toddler." Beatrice chuckled as she left the room without turning around.

There they sat: one energetic child waving crumbs onto the bed and one horrified child wondering if she could survive ten hours alone with her daughter. Then, a most disturbing thought entered Cordelia's mind, *How am I to shower?*

Not surprisingly, Cordelia religiously showered every night and every morning. Ophy's presence made that impossible. But when she looked at her daughter's dirty, chocolate-smudged face and hands, Cordelia had a horrifying thought: she'd need to bathe the child. Cordelia abhorred baths, as they defeated the purpose of ensuring one's own cleanliness by sitting in one's filth.

Later, in the early days of their relationship, when Aubrey had seductively suggested they should take a bath together, Cordelia had told her in no uncertain terms that was a deal-breaker. Now, she had no choice but to do that with Ophy, though once she drained the bathwater, she awkwardly held the child under the shower to wash off as much of the *ick* as possible.

Once somewhat cleansed, Cordelia had to figure out the next nine-and-a-half hours.

"Have you eaten, then?" Cordelia asked Ophy.

"No."

What kind of grandmother gives chocolate biscuits to a child but no breakfast?

When they went to the kitchen, there was no one there. Much to Cordelia's irritation, Beatrice had given Flora the day off.

Up in the highchair went Ophy—lest she escape while Cordelia searched for something to feed her. While Cordelia had never actually fed the child herself, she knew that Ophy liked cereal. Out came the Weetabix, milk, and sugar, and, for good measure, she cut up a banana to give to her. Inexperienced parent that she was, she forgot to bib Ophy, and by the end of breakfast, Ophy was a mess again.

Back to the bath Ophy unhappily went, which she expressed by crying the entire time. It was only 10:00 a.m., and Cordelia was already exhausted.

They spent the next few hours coloring, playing with dolls, and, most horrifyingly, sculpting extremely abstract art with Play-Doh. In between wiping Ophy's hands with wet wipes and taking her to her potty chair, which required Cordelia to do unmentionable things, Cordelia cursed her mother and ate English butter toffee candies, which she unwisely pinched off pieces of to give to her child.

As if Ophy had not ingested enough sugar already, Cordelia then made her a nut butter and strawberry jam sandwich and cut up apple slices for lunch—she did, however, remember to bib Ophy, so only a thorough wet wipes scrubbing of hands and face was needed.

After lunch, Cordelia mistakenly believed it was nap time. Ophy had other ideas and screamed at the top of her lungs that she wasn't sleepy and/or wailed. To the living room they went, where Cordelia put on her least favorite form of entertainment, *Teletubbies*.

On one of their many trips back to the potty chair, Cordelia snatched the sash from her robe, tied hers and Ophy's wrists to it, and then proceeded to lie on the couch. When Beatrice, Portia, and Miranda returned to the house at six o'clock, they found Cordelia passed out there with Ophy sleeping atop her chest. The room was an unmitigated disaster, with toys, Play-Doh, and wet wipes everywhere.

Beatrice gently roused Cordelia. "Darling, wake up."

Cordelia jerked up, fearful that Ophy had somehow unbound herself. When she saw that it was only her mother and that her daughter was still soundly sleeping, she whispered, "My God, Mother, you are a saint."

This elicited a soft chuckle from Beatrice. "No, Darling, just a mother."

* * *

During her last week in St. Albans, Cordelia paid particular attention to what Ms. Johnson and Beatrice fed Ophy, how they kept her entertained, and, most importantly, how to soothe her when she became irritable. Beatrice saw that her daughter was *finally* interested in how one took care of a child. She also noticed that her daughter's fondness for drink had dramatically dissipated. Both of these things warmed her heart.

As they walked to the door to say their goodbyes, Beatrice hesitantly asked, "We will see you at Christmastime, correct?"

Cordelia was offended by the question. "Of course, Mother. A deal is a deal." And then, after a long pause, she asked, "Might I expect a call from you and…Ophy on Sunday morning?"

This was music to Beatrice's ears.

"If that's what you want, Darling—provided you are prepared for such a call."

Cordelia knew her mother's meaning: 'Don't be hungover when we call.'

"I would *prefer* nothing more than to awake to your lecturing… and guidance, Mother."

* * *

Late August 2008: St. Albans, England

No mother wanted their daughter to be happy more than Beatrice Wainwright. The sheer, absolute hell that Cordelia had put her through with dumping Ophy at her feet and then almost killing herself with pills and drink because of it would've made some mothers consider severing the cord completely. Yet, she felt she bore some of the blame for her daughter's extremely poor life decisions.

Yes, Beatrice had tried her best to push Cordelia out of the nest and acknowledge that she herself was a mother bird. Still, she'd also swooped in way too many times when her fledgling seemed utterly unable to fully take care of herself, let alone her own fledgling. Moreover, she knew it was useless to shame Cordelia into acknowledging Ophy as her own because her daughter's shame was the exact reason she was *still Dilly* to the eight-year-old girl she absolutely adored.

For sixteen weeks out of the year, Cordelia was as content as she would allow herself to be. She did whatever Ophy wanted without question or complaint, even *horrid* things like riding horses and attending various children's shows—in crowded theaters with other screaming, germ-infested children nonetheless. Her unconditional, yet undeclared, love for Ophy *finally* made her somewhat normal, greatly pleasing Beatrice. However, there are fifty-two weeks in a year.

Although it didn't need to be confirmed, what with their terse weekly Sunday morning chats, Geoffrey and Mrs. Holt kept Beatrice apprised of just how miserable, guilt-ridden, and lonely her workaholic daughter was the other thirty-six weeks of the year.

Other than Bradley, Cordelia had no friends, and she never left her *bloody sterilized laboratory* of a house to go anywhere other than to work. And, most troubling of all, Cordelia *still* hadn't found someone who could make her want to do anything more than sleep in her bed—*alone*. Beatrice was convinced that if Cordelia could open herself up to the possibility of sharing intimacy, and, dare she say it, *love*, with another woman, then she could also reconsider her stance on assuming her rightful place as Ophy's mother—and, not just for sixteen weeks out of the year.

Just when Beatrice had almost lost all hope of this ever happening, Geoffrey rang her to pass along a message to Cordelia, who'd rudely told him 'not to bloody fucking ring' her while she was on holiday, about the progress her new co-star was making with her dialect coach. Although she had little interest in watching her daughter's dark and depressing films, Beatrice was keenly interested in learning everything there was to know about the other women who worked with Cordelia on those same films—namely, were any of them dark-haired, attractive lesbians with sexy legs.

"Geoffrey just rang, Delia," Beatrice said nonchalantly as she walked into her daughter's bedroom without knocking.

Cordelia irritably looked up from the black, gold-inlaid pigeonhole desk where she was scribbling into her Letts' planner. "I told him not to bother me! What did he want, then?"

"Oh, not much," Beatrice said as she sat on her daughter's neatly made bed. Then she trained her eyes on Cordelia's back. "He asked me to tell you that your new co-star is progressing well with Peggy. You've been here nearly three months, Darling; why haven't you mentioned that you had to replace Emma Jones at the last minute?"

There was a slight, perceptible flinch, and then, without turning around, Cordelia cut through the snare her mother was attempting to set for her with a machete.

"She is my subordinate, Mother. And, whatever scenario you have cooked up in your silly and hopeful mind, should be immediately thrown into the rubbish bin."

Her daughter's direct need to disavow her of her 'silly hopes' told Beatrice all she needed to know: *She fancies this girl!*

"Hmm…that's a pity, Darling," Beatrice feigned a sigh as she rose from the bed and walked over toward the desk, where she bent down and kissed Cordelia's forehead and said in a pitying tone, "because Geoffrey says that her full, pouty lips practically beg to be kissed and that she has a pair of legs that anyone would die to have wrapped around them."

CHAPTER SIXTEEN

"Cordy"

Sept. 21, 2008: Irvine, CA

There was no need to quickly shut off her alarm, which went off every Sunday morning at six-thirty because Cordelia was wide awake and staring at the bare back of the woman who'd done things to her body that she'd only ever imagined in her dreams. She much *preferred* the real thing. And, while she would've enjoyed nothing more than to wake Aubrey up and beg her to do it all over again, there was the irritating matter of Beatrice's weekly inquisition to deal with.

She knew that her mother suspected she was attracted to Aubrey before being ordered to invite her for dinner, because Beatrice made it a point to ask her daughter every week how things were 'progressing with *Nightingales*'—Beatrice never asked about her films.

So, begrudgingly, Cordelia left the object of her desire, sleeping soundly in her bed, gathered up Aubrey's hastily discarded clothes, and went to the laundry room to wash them and wait for Beatrice's call.

Cordelia didn't know what to think when her cell phone didn't ring promptly at seven o'clock, as it did *every bloody week*. As she could only wait for it to ring and for Aubrey's clothes to finish washing, she went into the kitchen and turned on the coffeemaker. Then, she drank two cups of coffee and returned to the laundry room. The clock on her phone read 7:30 a.m., which Cordelia found disconcerting since it wasn't like Beatrice to be tardy. So, for the first time in many years, she was the one who rang her mother.

"Good morning, Darling," Beatrice cheerfully answered.

"Has something happened, Mother?" Cordelia anxiously asked.

"God, I hope so!" Beatrice exclaimed.

"What? Why did you not ring me this morning, Mother? For fuck's sake, I thought something might have happened at home," Cordelia said irritatedly.

Beatrice chuckled. "No, nothing new has happened here… but I had hoped that something quite extraordinarily *new* had happened over there."

Silence.

"Hmm…don't be angry with your mummy, Darling. I didn't ring because I thought you might be…otherwise engaged…Is that the washer sounding it is finished?" Beatrice bewilderedly asked when she heard the washer buzz. "When did you start doing your own laundry, Delia?"

Cordelia didn't know how to answer her mother without revealing that there was a naked woman presently sleeping in her bed. "Right, well…" she stammered.

Her perplexed state was all Beatrice needed to hear to get her answer.

"If you're doing *her* laundry, she must have done quite a lot for you and your poor, neglected body, Darling."

"Mother!" Cordelia embarrassedly shrieked, as her entire body felt as if it were burning brighter than a bonfire.

Although she couldn't see it, Beatrice stated what she knew to be a fact. "Stop blushing, Darling. There's nothing to be embarrassed about...*except* the fact that you left a naked woman in your bed to do her laundry and chat with your mummy," Beatrice joked.

Silence.

"So, you don't have to tell Mummy the down and dirty—God forbid!—but can you say, either with words or grumbles, whether you...*enjoyed* yourself?" Beatrice delicately asked.

Still blushing, Cordelia answered both her mother's question and prayers. "Yes, Mother, *multiple* times."

It was all Beatrice could do not to shout, 'Thank you, Jesus!' Instead, she asked even more delicately, "And...what about her?"

This conversation was already uncomfortable enough, but now her mother wanted Cordelia to admit her own inadequacies!

"I...have a lot to learn, Mother," she stammered.

At this, Beatrice softly laughed. "Yes, Darling, you *most* certainly do."

* * *

Early Jan. 2010: St. Albans, England

While it was never openly discussed just precisely what Cordelia had learned when it came to pleasing Aubrey in bed, Beatrice knew from Mrs. Holt that the 'lovebirds' had, for the most part, a healthy sex life. Yes, there were nights when Aubrey would sleep in that ridiculous house next door, but she always came back to Cordelia's bed. So, that missing link in the chain of Cordelia's adult development was safely secured.

Yet, it troubled Beatrice that her daughter *still* hadn't openly acknowledged that she'd been cohabitating with Aubrey since the previous spring. She'd wanted Cordelia to bring Aubrey home to meet the Wainwrights the previous summer. Had she not seemed so, dare she say it, *happy*, Beatrice might have chastised her daughter for treating the girl like her mistress—sneaking off to call her and hastily ending their conversations whenever someone walked into a room where they could overhear a very different tone in her voice.

But when Cordelia returned home for Christmastime this year, that tone was replaced by another, very distressing one: Doubt. Beatrice knew something had changed between the 'lovebirds' when Cordelia walked into the house. Cordelia was clearly distracted and agitated by whatever occurred before she left Los Angeles.

First, Cordelia was unusually quiet—*even for her*. Two, she drank three to four glasses of wine every night at dinner— Beatrice hadn't seen her consume alcohol, other than a glass of champagne on New Year's Eve, in nearly seven years. Third, she'd seen her daughter pop an extra 'happy pill' on more than one occasion during her three-week stay in St. Albans. Fourth, and most importantly, Beatrice called Mrs. Holt, who told her what happened before she and Cordelia left for England.

All these things combined told Beatrice that her daughter was on the verge of doing something *completely stupid*. Before Cordelia could totally blow up her well-constructed plan—*Operation Make Cordelia Normal*—Beatrice stepped in with the help of Portia and Miranda.

After returning from dropping Ophy at St. Mary's, Cordelia found all of the other Wainwright women waiting for her at the dining table. She didn't like the determined looks on their faces as she uneasily took her chair.

"'*So foul and fair a day I have not seen.*' Where is the wine, then, Witch One?" Cordelia sarcastically asked her mother when she couldn't find the wine sitting in its usual place on the table.

Beatrice was not amused and refused to be baited by her daughter's sarcasm.

"I thought we might have *one* clear-headed dinner before you returned home to *Aubrey*."

Usually, Cordelia would have been embarrassed by Beatrice's unwanted references to her rarely discussed relationship with another woman. Still, she was in a particularly foul mood after leaving Ophy in Cambridge.

"You assume a lot, Mother, for someone who is told so little."

Now, Beatrice knew that Cordelia was *definitely* about to do something *completely stupid*.

"I know you think you're as difficult to read as Shakespeare, Darling, but I assure you that your actions, words, and face read more like Dr. Seuss."

Glowering Silence.

"Hmm…your sisters and I *know* that you're not the cheating type, so that's obviously not the issue…but perhaps she has strayed?" Beatrice uneasily suggested.

"For fuck's sake, Mother! Contrary to popular belief, I can more than satisfy her needs!" This was said both vehemently and heatedly.

Both Miranda and Portia giggled at their sister's open admission that she was, in fact, a lesbian, but their giggles quickly stopped when Beatrice glared at them. Then she turned her attention back to Cordelia.

"Satisfying a woman sexually is not the same thing as satisfying her emotionally, Delia. *Most* women need more than that, and I expect Aubrey to be one of them.

"While we have not been *permitted* to see for ourselves, we can only assume that she loves you—otherwise, she would've left you and your myriad of issues long ago. Is *that* the issue?"

"The issue is that…she's changed, and I'm not sure I like it. I think it might be best—" Cordelia stammered.

But her mother cut her off at the knees before Cordelia could finish saying what Beatrice didn't want to hear.

"Nonsense! How *exactly* has she changed?" Beatrice pointedly demanded.

"Well, if you must know, she's become quite bossy—and not just in…bed. She wants to replace my furniture and tell her parents we live together. And she wants us to argue and demands that I buy her gifts," Cordelia indignantly explained.

At this, all three Wainwright women burst into riotous laughter, which only fueled Cordelia's indignation.

"I don't think it's fucking funny! When I met her, she was such an agreeable girl, and now she wants to completely change the dynamics of our relationship."

"That's exactly *IT*!" Beatrice exclaimed, pointing a very rude finger at her oldest daughter. "She's stood up to you, and you don't like it because you are used to having everything your own bloody way over there.

"You snap your well-manicured fingers, and your minions, enablers, and props do whatever you bloody well want. And, now, she's told you that's not how *two grown women* interact in a healthy *adult* relationship.

"What *else* did she tell you needed to change?"

More Glowering Silence.

"Hmm...what do you think, girls?" Beatrice knowingly looked at Miranda and Portia. "What might you expect from a man you've been sleeping with for more than a year...or living with since last March?"

Miranda got the first stab in. "I'd expect to have *met his family* ages ago."

Portia's blade was next. "I'd expect to spend all of our holidays together."

Beatrice smiled at her two well-adjusted daughters, and then, in unison, all three Wainwrights turned the metaphorical knife. "I'd expect *love!*"

"Why do I suddenly feel as though I am no longer in St. Albans but in the Roman Senate?" Cordelia asked with derision in her voice.

"Things didn't end well for that dictator, did they, Darling?" Beatrice quipped. Then her voice turned deathly serious. "For once in your miserable life, please heed Mummy's advice: do exactly what Aubrey asks—"

"But—"

"No buts, Delia! Although you refuse to admit it to us—and I expect to her, and God knows most of all to yourself—she makes you happy...adjacent.

"We are all painfully aware that your first inclination is to run from emotional attachments, but we've also seen you...evolve when it comes to Ophy. So, Darling, for the love of all that is holy, let Aubrey teach you that the greatest gift you could ever give to her—or yourself—'*is to love and be loved in return.*'"

* * *

Late August 2010: St. Albans, England

After sending Aubrey with Portia, Miranda, and Ophy to town to watch *Toy Story 3*, Beatrice went to Cordelia's bedroom. She found her sitting at Henry's black, gold-inlaid pigeonhole desk, scribbling in her Letts' planner.

She'd spent the last three months watching her oldest daughter very intently to see what progress had been made in her *Operation Make Cordelia Normal* scheme.

While the first week of Aubrey's visit didn't instill in Beatrice much confidence that her daughter would ever change, things started to look up once Aubrey explicitly told Cordelia what she wanted and expected—and miraculously, Cordelia did as she was told. It was apparent to anyone who watched them who ruled the roost. Her attire may have consisted of short skirts and dresses, but Aubrey *definitely* wore the pants in the relationship.

While they were not outwardly affectionate to one another around the family, Beatrice would occasionally see her daughter's hand find its way onto Aubrey's leg at the dining table or when they were sitting on the living room couch. But while there weren't welcome home or goodbye kisses, there were heart-warming smiles and terms of endearment. The first time she heard Cordelia refer to Aubrey as '*My Love*,' Beatrice had hastily retreated so her daughter didn't see her tears of happiness.

The Ophy-Aubrey dynamic dramatically changed once Cordelia told her daughter the truth about her relationship with Aubrey. It helped that Aubrey allowed Cordelia to sleep in Ophy's room at least twice a week and took Ophy into town to do whatever she wanted—which was usually spending Cordelia's money on sweets, books, and clothes. Aubrey's ability to turn a ten-year-old girl's jealousy into adoration convinced Beatrice that Aubrey was *definitely* mother material.

The adult Wainwright women also adored Aubrey. She was kind, intelligent, witty, and outgoing. Most importantly, she gave Cordelia's sisters and mother invaluable information about what went on in Los Angeles, at work, and at home. And, if she'd had one drink too many at lunch, she would occasionally provide insight into what really went on in their bedroom, too. She was *definitely* wife material.

With these things in mind, Beatrice watched her daughter's scribbling from the bedroom doorway and said, "I thought we might have a chat since the others have gone to town, *Cordy*."

Cordelia didn't look up but chuckled instead. "Hmm... *'Fair is foul, and foul is fair.'*"

Beatrice was not amused.

"Stop that scribbling, Darling. Mummy wants to have a grown-up conversation." She then walked over, sat on the bed, and waited for Cordelia to do as she was told.

After capping her pen, Cordelia obliged her mother and turned her desk chair to face the bed. "Yes, Mummy?" Cordelia smirked.

"What are your intentions toward this young woman, Delia?" Beatrice directly asked.

This time, Beatrice got a scoff. "You know I am the one who is your daughter, right?"

"Yes, Darling...but since you've brought up the subject of daughters, when do you plan on telling Aubrey about yours?"

Silence.

Beatrice knew that *Silence* meant *Never*. She didn't like that answer.

"I *know* that you love this woman, *Cordy*. No amount of sexual pleasure would allow you to let yourself be so skillfully managed by someone."

Then Beatrice stood, walked to the desk, and placed her mother's wedding ring on it. "This is the woman for you, Darling. Try not to muck it up because I cannot wait another decade for you to be human again. My mother's ring should not be given under false pretenses; do you *understand* me?" Beatrice pointedly looked at her daughter.

Cordelia passingly glanced at the ring but didn't pick it up. "Yes, Mother…but might this not be given to Portia instead? I am already married and—"

Beatrice was having none of it and curtly cut her off. "Nonsense! You are the oldest child, and it is either yours to wear or, in your case, to give.

"Never in my wildest dreams or prayers could I have envisioned Aubrey. She is the epitome of the perfect woman for you, and I *refuse* to let you sabotage or run away from that fact."

To answer her mother's vehemence, Cordelia unlocked the desk's middle drawer, picked up the ring, unceremoniously tossed it in, and relocked it.

"I *prefer* things as they are presently. Now is not the right time to tell her…things."

Her outrage could not be contained. "Goddamnit, Cordelia! Your *daughter* is ten years old—the right time has long passed. I allowed it before because you weren't…capable of doing it on your own, but *now* you have a good, loving woman who can help you raise her. For the love of God, please tell Aubrey the truth and live a happy, normal life," Beatrice passionately implored her daughter. "I cannot morally go along with this farce any longer, Delia."

At this, Cordelia angrily stood and slammed her hands onto the desk. "I'm not ready…*yet*! I'm not willing to gamble what I have right now with either the woman that I love or my daughter. I wouldn't survive it, Mother, if either of them hated me for… the person I once was. Please let me be happy for once in my miserable life!"

Like so many times before, Beatrice allowed her love for her daughter to blind her from doing the right thing. Perhaps it was the fact that Cordelia had finally called Ophy her daughter or that she openly admitted that she was in love and, most importantly, happy, but Beatrice agreed to stay silent until Cordelia was *finally* ready to grow up and take responsibility for her own decisions.

Of course, Beatrice didn't think it would take Cordelia another six years to do this.

* * *

June 2016: St. Albans, England

"And that, Ophelia, is my confession. Had I been a *much* better person, I would have told you I was your mother the minute you came home that day. But I was…selfish, and I was wrong, and for that and so many other things, I am truly sorry," Cordelia firmly admitted.

The Wainwright dining room was filled with complete silence and five female faces staring intently at Cordelia's. Portia, Miranda, and Beatrice had never heard her speak so openly and honestly about her failings as a mother and human being. Aubrey, of course, had spent the last six months listening to her wife tearfully confess all of her sins and regrets.

For Ophy, however, it was utterly shocking to hear the person she loved and admired most admit that she was the villain in the sordid story of *The Curious Case of Cordelia Wainwright.* No one made her abandon and then lie to Ophy for sixteen years. In fact, she had been the mastermind behind the crime and had made the other four women sitting at the table her unwilling accomplices.

"And, what am I supposed to say to this? That I forgive you, and we will *act* like you aren't a horrible person?" Ophy bitterly asked.

Cordelia weakly smiled at her daughter's indignation. "My *acting* days are over, Darling. For better or worse, I am your mother. What you choose to do about that is your choice.

"But I will tell you the same thing that my mother said not once but twice to me: I have done my best to teach you right from wrong, and now you must decide for yourself. I hope to God that you listen to your mother better than I did to mine. Trust me, Darling, when I tell you that you will be a much happier person for it."

Seeing an opportunity to lighten the room's mood, Beatrice quipped, "And, here, I thought you never listened to anything I ever said to you, Delia."

At this, all six women in the room laughed.

After a moment of reflection, Ophy looked at Cordelia and asked, "What should I call you then? Dilly or Mother?"

As relief washed over her that her daughter had more sense than she ever did and had made the right choice, Cordelia smiled. "Whichever you *prefer*, Darling."

* * *

Feb. 21, 2017: Irvine, CA

When Cordelia woke up, reality immediately set in. Today was the day she would tell the world who she really was, with a few minor details left out to protect Bradley and Ophy.

While she wished Bradley was ready like she was to admit that he was just a normal human being who *preferred* to sleep with people of his own sex, she knew that was his truth to tell and not hers.

As for Ophy, the Wainwrights had decided that it wasn't necessary to announce to the world that Cordelia had kept a child in the dark about her true parentage for most of her life. It was enough that they all knew and accepted the truth. And, while Ophy chose to refer to her mother as 'Dilly,' it didn't mean that Cordelia wasn't her mother. Because as the Bard wrote, '*What's in a name? That which we call a rose by any other name would smell just as sweet.*' The naming of things is irrelevant. It is our actions that define who we are.

Of course, no one was happier than Aubrey that after more than eight years of pretending that the love of her life was nothing more than a friend and business partner, she would *finally* be able to shout to the world, "That crazy bitch is into me!"

It was also most convenient because Aubrey was six months pregnant and tired of the press asking her if she would ever reveal who gave her the platinum two-carat solitaire wedding ring she wore on her left hand.

"I can feel those beautiful blue eyes of yours staring at me, *mi amor*," Aubrey softly said as she opened her eyes and turned to face her wife. "Am I to be treated to another *hot* shower and *naughty words* this morning?"

At this, Cordelia laughed. "No, *My Love*, it would not be proper in your condition...and if you fell on me in the shower, you might break my neck."

"Cordy!" Aubrey said offended, as she reached and jabbed Cordelia's propped-up elbow. "That's rude, even for you. Say you're sorry!" she demanded.

"Hmm...what should I be sorry for, then?" Cordelia asked as she feigned indignation. "You know, I used to *prefer* it much more when you only bossed me about in bed, Sweetheart...but, over the years, I have grown to appreciate your telling me what to do.

"Much like our friend Bartleby, I was starving myself to death—not from sausage rolls or English toffee pudding—but from what I needed most: love.

"Without your telling me that I *really, really, really* liked you, I would still be fantasizing about what it would feel like to kiss your soft, pouty lips and to have your long, curvy legs wrapped around mine. Ms. Wainwright was drowning in loneliness before she met you.

"Your stubborn, unyielding resolve forced me to do the proper *adult* things, like say: 'I was wrong, I am sorry, and I love you.' You *cured* me of all my *afflictions*.

"And now, whenever I am alone with you, you make me feel like I am not only Home, Whole, Young, Fun, and Free, but, most importantly, *Clean* again. And, for all those things—and so many more—I will always love you.

"So, will that suffice as an apology, *My Love*? Or will I need to throw out my current toothbrush?" Cordelia asked as she gave her wife a heartbreakingly beautiful smile.

Aubrey didn't know what to say or do except choke back her tears and say the first thing that came to mind: "I'm going to speak, and you're going to listen, got it? Nod your head if you understand."

Cordelia dutifully nodded.

"Cordy, you *will* kiss my soft, pouty lips right now—they *desperately* need yours," Aubrey rasped.

* * *

Feb. 21, 2017: Hollywood, CA

"That's not exactly true, Cordelia. Your recent divorce from Bradley Simpson has certainly made headlines. You two seemed so happy, and then, poof, after fourteen years of marriage, it was over. What happened?" Patti asked.

After a long moment of reflection on this very impertinent and rude question, *Cordy* smiled—a true, non-camera-ready, beaming smile—and spoke Her Truth.

"*As You Like It*, then, Patti. For most of my life, all the world was a stage, and Bradley was one of the many players on it. He promptly entered my life on cue when I needed him most, and now he has chosen to exit Stage Left when I no longer need him to 'prop' me up.

"An actress, just like any real woman, plays many roles in her time. When I was twenty-three, I needed to play the part of a happy young woman in love with her husband because I was a miserable young girl who hated herself.

"But, '*as good luck would have it*,' at age twenty-eight, I met the absolute most beautiful, though way too fidgety, woman I had ever seen. She saw behind my curtain and forced me to stand centre stage and say my lines honestly for once in my miserable life: that I so *desperately* wanted to be with her—and those goddamn sexy legs of hers.

"And, while it has taken me way too many *Acts* to acknowledge that I would have quite literally died had she exited Stage Right at the beginning of my Third Act, I am *finally* ready '*to thine own self be true*' and admit that I unequivocally love and adore my 'BFF' and wife, *Mrs.* Aubrey Taylor-Wainwright.

"It has been said that no one takes direction like me. And, while I may be the greatest actress Aubrey knows, she is *most* assuredly my greatest director—though, my mother deserves an assistant directing credit, too.

"Aubrey made me grow up—and, most importantly, she *demanded* that I stop *acting* like an adult and a human and actually become them. And, so I did, and now I have assumed the most significant role of my life: Wife and Mother.

"So, yes, 2017, is the year that I *finally* get what I most covet."

Interview Over

Bella Books
Happy Endings Live Here
P.O. Box 10543
Tallahassee, FL 32302
Phone: (800) 729-4992
www.BellaBooks.com

More Titles from Bella Books

Jones – Gerri Hill
978-1-64247-598-2 | 260 pages | Mystery
One weekend getaway, six friends, and a deadly secret that will wash away everything they thought they knew.

Merry Weihnachten – E. J. Noyes
978-1-64247-610-1 | 292 pages | Romance
Christmas traditions aren't the only things getting mixed up when these two hearts collide beneath the mistletoe.

Sweet Home Alabarden Park – TJ O'Shea
978-1-64247-570-8 | 362 pages | Romance
She came to restore a royal estate—she never expected to rebuild her heart.

Dr. Margaret Morgan – Christy Hadfield
978-1-64247-628-6 | 286 pages | Romance
Facing the professor on campus everyone hates is terrifying—but falling for her might be even worse.

Overtime – Tracey Richardson
978-1-64247-630-9 | 278 pages | Romance
A charming romance about second chances, found family, and scoring the goal that matters most.

The Big Guilt – Renée J. Lukas
978-1-64247-657-6 | 206 pages | Romance
What if the one who got away became the one you can't have?

www.ingramcontent.com/pod-product-compliance
Lightning Source LLC
Chambersburg PA
CBHW020633110726
47899CB00002B/764